"I'm Sure I Can Count On Your Discretion, Anna."

Reynaldo narrowed his eyes and added, "Neither of us wants our parents to be the subject of prurient gossip."

"Oh, really?" she said. "Perhaps your father gave my mom those jewels to buy her silence. Paid her to be invisible, a nobody. A secret mistress." She rose to her feet, heart pounding, and threw her napkin on the table next to her untouched dessert. "Well, I'm ashamed to know you. Any of you DeLeons."

"You don't understand the situation." His icy voice chilled her.

"I understand all I need to," she said. Fists clenched against the onslaught of all she'd learned and couldn't even begin to process, she rushed from the dining room, tugged open the heavy front door and flew down the stone steps.

He didn't come after her. She hadn't expected him to. He knew she'd be back for her money.

She knew it, too. And that made the long, dusty moonlit walk back to the cottage more grueling than ever.

Dear Reader,

What is it about an inheritance, or even the hope of one, that can make otherwise sane people lose their minds? I don't know how many stories I've heard about relatives who are so incensed by the idea that someone else might get Grandma's good silver or Aunt Alice's heirloom quilt that they start plotting and sneaking and running around in a panic to secure what is "rightfully" theirs—often while poor Aunt Alice is still alive and well.

As a writer I do pity my characters for the sticky situations I like to throw them into. It was quite wicked of me to take an inheritance the deliciously arrogant Naldo has been expecting his whole life and give a little piece of it to his childhood playmate, Anna. I knew it would make them both crazy, but—what can I say? I couldn't resist the temptation.

I hope you enjoy Anna and Naldo's story.

Best,

Jennifer Lewis

JENNIFER LEWIS

SEDUCED FOR THE INHERITANCE

Published by Silhouette Books
America's Publisher of Contemporary Romance

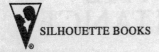

SILHOUETTE BOOKS

ISBN-13: 978-0-373-76830-1
ISBN-10:   0-373-76830-3

SEDUCED FOR THE INHERITANCE

Visit Silhouette Books at www.eHarlequin.com

Printed in U.S.A.

Books by Jennifer Lewis

Silhouette Desire

The Boss's Demand #1812
Seduced for the Inheritance #1830

JENNIFER LEWIS

has been dreaming up stories for as long as she can
remember and is thrilled to be able to share them with
readers. She has lived on both sides of the Atlantic and
worked in media and the arts before she grew bold
enough to put pen to paper. She is happily settled in
New York with her family, and would love to hear from
readers at jen@jen-lewis.com.

For the Brainstorming Desirables, the most helpful, friendly, supportive and fun group of writers I know.

Acknowledgments:

Massive thanks to everyone who read this book while I was writing it, including Anne, Anne-Marie, Carol, Cynthia, Deb, Leeanne, Marie, Mel and Paula.

One

"What are you doing here?" A commanding voice and a pair of black eyes pierced the evening gloom from inside the tiny cottage.

It was him.

She'd known she'd see Reynaldo De Leon sooner or later—it was his estate, after all—but she'd wanted to be psyched up and dressed for success, not sweaty, disheveled and emotional from a day of sorting through her beloved mother's belongings.

Anna Marcus's fingers tightened around her bag of greasy take-out food.

He stared down at her from his impressive height. A crease appeared between black brows. "Have you come to clean?"

He looked huge in the cramped kitchen, the single dim bulb illuminating his arrogant features, his wide, sensual mouth tilted with disdain. "If you're getting paid by the hour I'll reimburse you for tonight, but you must tell your employer to get in touch with me before any property is removed."

He thinks I'm a cleaner? Did he not recognize her?

Suddenly it was all too much to bear. Her gentle mother dead at only forty-eight, with no warning at all, just a late-night phone call about an accident on a Florida interstate—

"Well?" He crossed his arms over his expensive shirt.

Tears welled in her eyes. *Don't cry now.* In the last year she'd survived bankruptcy, divorce and now the loss of the one person in the world she could always count on. She'd made it this far....

The bag in her hand crinkled as she clutched it tighter, biting hard on the inside of her mouth.

"*No habla inglés?*" He raised a black brow.

"I speak English," she blurted.

"That bag is leaking."

"What?" She followed his gaze to the brown paper bag in her hand. "Oh, it's my dinner."

His hard expression softened. "Go ahead and eat it." He gestured to the Formica-topped table. "No sense letting food go to waste."

Maybe she could play along until he left? Let him think she really was some minimum-wage cleaner. What did it matter? Neither he nor his high-and-mighty father had bothered to come to her mom's funeral, despite the fact that Letty Marcus lived on the estate and cooked all their meals for more than fifteen years. Working stiffs like her and her mom were nobody to these people.

Yes, she had a college degree, and had briefly owned a successful real estate company, but right now she was flat broke, with no place to call home, so his assessment of her wasn't all that wide of the mark.

As she grabbed a plate off the counter and sat at the table, she could feel his eyes on her. Eyes that had haunted her teenage dreams and driven her into frenzies of pathetic hope that one day he'd…

Love her?

What a joke. She lifted her big Quarter Pounder with cheese out of the bag and plopped it on the plate.

She sat in the chair and picked up the burger, then realized her stomach had shriveled to the size of a peanut. His imperious gaze made her skin prickle. "Are you going to stand there watching me?"

"Of course. I can't leave a stranger unattended on family property. Surely you understand."

A stranger? She wasn't sure whether to laugh or cry or scream.

Just one more insignificant person on a large estate. No one special. He probably hadn't spared a thought for her since the last time they faced each other on the tennis court.

She'd thought about him, though. Far more than she cared to admit.

Dropping the burger on her plate, she rose onto unsteady legs. "I have to go."

Naldo reached into his back pocket and took a twenty-dollar bill from his money clip. "Here. You can come back tomorrow."

After I've found what I'm looking for.

"I don't want your money." She kept her head turned away from him. "And I'm not hungry. You can eat it."

Naldo fought a smile at the thought of eating the cleaner's greasy take-out dinner. There was a fresh-boiled lobster waiting for him back at the house.

Not that he had any appetite today.

He looked around for a piece of paper to write his number. If he could put off the cleaner for one more day he'd be fine. He'd find what he was looking for tonight. The cottage was tiny.

The girl hadn't bothered to respond, so he simply scribbled the number on a heart-shaped notepad next to the phone and held it out to her. A bead of sweat balanced like a tiny pearl above her pursed pink mouth.

As she took the pink paper, her soft fingertips brushed his palm, sparking a strange sensation. Her eyes met his, wide and blue, and recognition swept through him like a clap of thunder.

"Anna."

Her chin jerked up.

He stared at her for a moment, not quite able to trust his eyes. How could this skinny, nervous woman be the feisty tomboy he'd once known? "It's been a long time."

"Apparently so." Her pale lips pressed together.

"You look so different." The words flew out before he had time to consider their prudence.

"Time will do that to a person. To some people anyway. You look exactly the same."

"You're so thin."

"It's the fashion." Her eyes narrowed.

"Your hair, it used to be red."

"It still is, until I lighten it."

"You dye your hair?" It seemed inconceivable that the tough and boyish Anna he remembered would do something so unabashedly feminine.

"Don't look so shocked. Most women do."

"You never were like most women."

"Who says I am now?" Her eyes flashed.

The old fire was still there, just in a very different vessel. And it sparked more than curiosity.

"I hear you're a big success." Her mother's pride had kept him well-versed in Anna's accomplishments: magna cum laude graduation from a good college, a job with a top developer, a venture in commercial real estate.

A husband.

"It's all relative. Success, that is. I hear the estate has branched out into retail." Her voice was cool, controlled. The voice of a businesswoman. Intriguingly at odds with her disheveled appearance.

"Yes, citrus-based marinades, salad dressings, dipping sauces. They're selling well."

She held his gaze. "I'm sure the De Leon citrus empire will thrive for another four hundred years."

Thank God she'd managed to change the subject. Terror streaked along her nerves when he touched on her "success." Whatever brief success she'd enjoyed lay in dust. Not unlike the dust that clung to her ratty cut-off shorts and faded T-shirt. Why did he have to see her looking her absolute worst? So tired, faded, drawn and scrawny, he didn't even know her. Her heart squeezed with shame.

"We're all devastated by your mother's death." The compassion in his eyes and the sincerity in his velvet voice *almost* made her forget that he didn't even show for her funeral.

She still couldn't believe her mom was really gone. That she'd never again sink into those soft, loving arms and relax in the warmth of love that was truly unconditional.

"Me, too." Her voice emerged as a whisper.

"My father died this morning." Naldo's deep voice rang with disbelief.

"What?" Robert De Leon was a force of nature, as tall, proud, sturdy and indestructible as the orange trees that grew in such profusion on the vast empire he ruled.

"A massive heart attack. He hung on for three days, but the doctors said there wasn't anything they could do for him."

"Oh, Naldo." Her hand flew to her mouth as fresh emotion burned through her.

His proud bearing belied the pain churning in his fierce black eyes. A sudden, violent urge to hug him almost knocked her off her feet.

Don't even think about it.

She'd always wanted Naldo De Leon. Craved his touch, his admiration—his love. She knew by now that she'd never have them. She wouldn't take this painful moment and turn it into an even more devastating one.

"The estate is yours now." She said it calmly, collecting herself.

"Yes."

"The four-hundred-year history of the De Leon plantation is an impressive legacy to continue. I know you'll make your father proud."

Naldo didn't reply. With the arrogance of the conquistadors he was descended from, he simply stared at her.

She groped for something else to say. To slice through the thundercloud of emotion thickening in the air. *Don't cry.*

She needed to get out of here. It had taken her two days to pluck up the courage to come at all, but apparently she still couldn't hack it.

"I guess you're ready to give the cottage to another employee, so I'll come back tomorrow to finish packing. I'm staying in town. I have to go." She realized she still clutched the heart-shaped piece of pink paper with his home phone number.

She'd never called him on the phone. Their relationship had been more a catch-as-catch-can affair. *Hey, wanna play some ball?* No planned assignations or formal invitations. They'd been "buddies" but never really friends in the true sense.

She left the number on the counter, picked up her burger and threw it in the black plastic trash bag she hadn't yet managed to bring herself to throw any of her mom's things into, then sucked in a breath and stepped toward the door. "It is okay if I come back tomorrow?"

Naldo's unmoving presence marked the fact that her mother's little cottage was *his* property. "Of course. Take all the time you need."

She waited for a moment longer, hoping for—what? A conversational foray? An invitation to join him for dinner?

Get over yourself, girl.

His impassive silence suggested he was waiting for her to leave, so she hurried out the door and climbed once more into the ancient battered van that had miraculously survived the drive down from Boston.

Hot tears blurred her view through the scarred windshield as she steered the van along the winding access road toward the estate's grand entrance. How many more times would she make this journey? One? Maybe two? Now her mom was gone she had no home and no one was waiting for her. But she was tough and she'd get it together and live a life that would make her mom proud.

Two days later, Anna shivered in the air-conditioned chill of the De Leon's grand living room as an inlaid walnut grandfather clock struck four. Strangers milled about, speaking in hushed tones, waiting for the reading to start. She'd received a phone call at the motel from a lawyer, asking her to attend the reading of Robert De Leon's will. The De Leons followed the old-school custom of providing small legacies for the staff, including her mother.

She had not been invited to the small, private funeral held that morning at the estate.

There was a sharp divide between the household staff, gathered for the occasion in their ordinary clothes, and the elegantly dressed family members also in attendance. Naldo stood among the latter, breathtaking in a fine black suit, his thick, wavy, almost-black hair combed back to reveal his dramatic features. If he'd noticed her, he showed no sign of it. Anna stood alone, off to one side, staring out the French windows at thousands of acres of the finest citrus groves in the world.

Today she was carefully dressed in a good suit and high heels. With earrings, makeup and an upswept hairdo she hoped she looked like the woman her mom had lovingly boasted about to the other staff.

"Ladies and gentlemen, please take your seats." A suited young man ushered them toward four rows of Queen Anne chairs she recognized as being filched from the dining room. She knew the house pretty well, at least the public rooms, though she'd spent most of her time hanging out in the kitchen while her mom prepped and cooked the family meals.

The lawyer's authoritative voice descended into a soft drone as he read the long list of bequests. All money, of course. The estate was legendary for never breaking off even the tiniest chunk of land, which was how it had remained intact for centuries. The eldest son—Naldo—got the land and the vast bulk of whatever monstrous holdings in gold and currency and other investments there were. His sister got some kind of stipend. Since she was at least ten years older than him and lived in Europe, Anna had never met her and couldn't even pick her out in the small knot of relatives.

She shifted in her chair, her uncomfortable slingbacks pinching her toes. Two thousand dollars and ten thousand dollars seemed to be the going rate for staff bequests. She suspected her mom would get the latter, due to her long service. Boy would that money be welcome! Her kindhearted mother had left her savings to a shelter for unwed mothers. She had no way of knowing that Anna was almost literally down to her last dime, which was in fact owed to the fleabag motel she was staying in.

"To Leticia Marcus, valued employee and treasured friend—" Anna sat up "—I leave her place of residence and the ground on which it stands, as demarcated on the attached map, and the book of recipes we developed together."

He'd moved on to the next bequest by the time it sank in.

No money at all?

Her heart plummeted.

A scraping sound drew her attention and everyone turned as Naldo rose to his feet. "What?" His deep voice trembled with barely controlled rage.

"Mr. De Leon, may I speak with you outside for a moment?" An older, grizzled member of the team of lawyers rose and indicated the door. Naldo strode to the door, fury pouring from him in a hot wave that rolled over the crowd and left excited whispering in its wake.

People turned and glanced surreptitiously at Anna. *The daughter*, she heard someone mutter. She swallowed and tried to hold her head high as a flush crept up her neck.

Why would Robert De Leon leave her mother a different legacy than he'd bequeathed to all the other staff members?

"You cannot be serious." Naldo paced in the hall, anger simmering just below boiling point. "My father would never have approved this."

"It was his expressed wish. I tried to talk him out of it myself. I tried to explain that the integrity of the estate—"

"The integrity of the estate? This bequest makes a mockery of the estate. The De Leon plantation has had no changes in its borders other than opportunistic expansion since my ancestors arrived here from Hispaniola in 1583. And now you mean to tell me that my father instructed you to carve a one-acre hole right in the middle of it? Why not give her one of my kidneys as well? It defies belief." He underscored his disbelief with a loud smack of his hand on the doorframe. The bespectacled functionary in front of him flinched.

"I'm sorry, sir, but I'm afraid it was your father's expressed intention. I'm sure you understand the exigencies of client confidentiality, but perhaps you are aware of the circumstances—"

"I'm aware of the *circumstances*."

My father's affair with Letty Marcus. A ten-year-long fly in the ointment of his existence and an ongoing affront to the memory of his mother.

He raked a hand through his hair. "Can nothing be done? Surely our ancestors never intended for something like this to happen."

"I imagine they are rotating in the family crypt as we speak, sir." The lawyer's smirk only stirred his irritation. "I would suggest that you talk to the daughter. I suspect that if you offer her the right amount of money—"

"She'll sell."

* * *

As the lawyers packed up their papers and the gathered audience rose to their feet, Naldo took in the chiseled elegance of Anna's profile, set off by the high chignon that held her pale gold hair. Skillfully applied makeup enhanced the symmetrical beauty of her fine features, and darkened that deliciously prim mouth. The tough little girl with the wild red hair and freckled nose had morphed into a stunning woman.

A woman he wouldn't mind spending some time with.

"Would you join me for dinner?"

Shock flickered through her beautiful eyes. "What?"

"The cook has some fine red snapper she's promised to grill to the exact point where it cooks in its juices but retains its tender plumpness." He couldn't ignore the tender plumpness of her pretty lower lip as she bit it.

"You have a new cook already?"

"Yes. She's not in your mother's league, of course—" *Perhaps mentioning the cook was a mistake.* "But one must make do."

"I can quite imagine." Was that a flare of annoyance he read in her expression?

He picked up her hand. Pale and soft, the nails short and bare but carefully contoured. With her long, slender fingers encased in his, again he experienced the shimmer of sensation that had preceded recognition at the cottage.

He lifted her hand to his mouth, and pressed his lips against the smooth skin. The absence of the expensive scent he'd expected to encounter only stirred his arousal. "Dine with me, Anna. With my father gone, I—" He held her gaze.

He needed her to say yes, and not just because the prospect of dinner without his father made his soul ache. He had a problem to solve, and suddenly he envisioned a few very delicious ways to solve it.

Two

"Okay." Anna regretted the word as soon as it left her lips, but she couldn't help it. She saw the fresh pain that glittered in Naldo's dark eyes. She knew how much he loved his father.

"Excellent." Was that a look of triumph that flashed across his face? Fear crept up her spine.

He gestured to a young man in black pants and a white shirt. "Mojitos on the veranda please, Tom."

With his hand still on hers—which was growing uncomfortably hot—he leaned into her and murmured, "I'll get rid of these last stragglers and join you outside."

Out on the veranda, with a drink she hadn't asked for sweating in her hand, Anna paced back and forth over the smooth painted wood.

Now she'd have to keep up her successful businesswoman charade for the length of a fancy meal. She couldn't let Naldo know what had happened. He'd no doubt pity her and laugh at her foolish pretensions to a lifestyle he took for granted.

She sipped her drink and the sharp lime and fresh mint stung her tongue—painful and delicious, their heady taste echoed the sharp mix of emotions still roiling inside her.

She hadn't realized how much she'd missed this place. She marveled at the endless rows of lush trees burgeoning under the clear bright blue sky, as the scent of ripe oranges thickened the air. The estate was known as Paradiso, and the name fit. A little piece of heaven.

Or a big piece of it, depending on your perspective.

And now a very, very tiny piece of it was hers.

"Anna!" She jumped as Naldo strode through the French doors. "I thought I'd never be rid of them."

He'd removed his tie and unbuttoned the neck of his white shirt, revealing a tantalizing glimpse of bronzed skin at his throat. He picked up his tall mojito glass from the table. For one second she was agonizingly aware of the long, powerful fingers that had held hers with such tender yet irresistible force. He lifted the glass, threw his head back and drank.

"God, what a day." He slammed the half-empty glass down on the table. He shrugged his expensive jacket off and threw it casually over a wicker chair. "Let me look at you."

She stood fixed to the spot as he—without any shame— let his eyes rove over her from head to toe, appearing to drink her in like a tall, cool mojito.

The warm approval in his gaze sparked a rush of sensation that stung her fingertips and nipples. She covered her confusion in a sip of her drink.

"Don't be shy. I'm just in shock, that's all. I can't believe that you're the tough cookie with the cropped hair who used to challenge me to arm-wrestling matches." Amusement twinkled in his eyes.

A rush of memories flooded her veins with that strange mix of pain and pleasure. "You used to let me win."

"I *never* let you win. You used to kick my ass regularly, until I grew bigger."

Until your mother died, and you didn't come home anymore.

She'd looked forward to his boarding school vacations with every cell in her body. He'd come home bursting with energy, thrilled to be back and up for anything. But after his mother's death he always had somewhere else to go—skiing in Aspen, polo in Argentina, a tour of Italy. She hadn't really seen him again after that. She was gone by the time he graduated from college and moved back here.

She shook off the thought of how suddenly he'd disappeared from her life. "I did always beat you at tennis, didn't I?" She remembered with a surge of pleasure how he could never take a set away from her.

"You were a menace on the courts. Do you still play?" His dark eyes sparkled.

"No." She sipped her drink quickly, to cover a rush of sadness. "I haven't had much time for that kind of thing since I left here."

"You know what they say about all work and no play. I can't get over how thin you are. What happened to all those tough muscles you were so proud of?"

They went the same way as the rest of my strength. Into a bad marriage and a worse business partnership.

She shrugged and forced a smile. "Life, you know."

"Your mother told me you got divorced. I'm sorry." The flash of pity in his eyes stuck her like a knife.

There had been no way to hide the failure of her marriage from the one person she trusted most in the world. At least her mom had never learned of the accompanying financial ruin.

"One of those things." She took another sip of her bittersweet drink. The liquor warmed her blood and softened the tension creeping through her. "Did you ever marry?"

"I think you know the answer to that question."

Strange relief crept through her. "No? You'll have to one day. The future of the De Leon dynasty depends on it."

"True. A weighty burden."

"Will you continue the tradition of importing a famously beautiful duke's daughter from Spain?" She still remembered how stunning his mother was, even in her fifties. Intimidating as hell, but undeniably gorgeous.

He sipped his refilled drink and she read something odd in his gaze. The hint of a challenge? "Perhaps I will. There's a lot to be said for tradition."

"Your father never remarried. Was he lonely?"

"I was with him." His brusque reply startled her.

"You were away at boarding school, then at college, for most of five years after your mom died."

His nostrils flared briefly. "I smell the snapper. Let's go inside."

He swept through the door, leaving a trail of unease in his wake.

What had she said?

An intimate table for two was set in the bright, cheery breakfast room. She'd always liked this spot better than the imposing main dining room, and right now it looked cozy and inviting. White wine glittered in crystal glasses and candlelight danced over shimmering silver cutlery and hand-painted porcelain. A young man served the steaming fish.

"Are these plates Chinese?"

"Yes, eighteenth century. My ancestor Francisco Alvaro De Leon brought them back from his travels in the Orient."

Even the plates around here had a pedigree dating back two hundred years. Not her. She'd never even met her own father.

She stuck her fork into the fish. Succulent juices flowed from the perfectly cooked flesh.

"You're in real estate?" He asked the question with warm curiosity. His pique of a few moments ago had vanished.

She took a deep breath. "My husband and I started a company buying and leasing commercial properties."

"Intriguing. That's a tough business. Your mother told me you did well for yourself."

"Yes." *For a while.* She couldn't bring herself to tell her mom what had really happened. "When we divorced we dissolved the company, though. I haven't decided what to do next."

The delicate flavor of the fish, lightly crusted with tangy spices, exploded over her tongue. "Your new cook is good." She felt like a traitor as she swallowed the delicious food and forked another bite.

Naldo paused in the act of raising his wineglass to his mouth and held her gaze as the candle flame danced in his penetrating eyes. "Your mother will be missed by all of us."

Anna swallowed. "I've been gone so long. So busy, and all the way up in Boston. I haven't been back as often as I'd—"

"She understood. Believe me, your success made her happier than you can know. She was so proud of you, always showing your letters to everyone and talking about your latest accomplishments."

Guilt speared into her. Still, she was glad her mom died believing her successful and solvent.

Naldo's smile revealed white teeth, perfectly even except for one slightly crooked incisor. A tiny imperfection that added distinctive charm. Why did he have to be so painfully handsome?

"You must be anxious to get back to Boston. I don't imagine a big, dusty farm holds much appeal now that you don't have any relations here." He punctuated his statement with a mouthful of fish.

"I hardly think of the De Leon estate as a big dusty farm."

"All right. A big sandy farm." Dark humor twinkled in his eyes. "Where nothing ever changes. Just blossoms blooming and oranges ripening. I guess that's not too exciting for a successful Boston businesswoman."

"I guess not." Unease roamed through her as she broke off a flake of fish with the tines of her fork.

The sensation of Naldo's hard gaze made her look up. He stared at her, eyes slightly narrowed, candlelight shimmering over the harsh planes of his handsome face.

Something tightened in her gut. What was he up to?

"Two hundred thousand dollars." His authoritative voice spoke the words like a command.

"What?"

"My price for the cottage."

"It can't be worth that much," she blurted before she came to her senses. Two hundred thousand dollars? Somewhere inside her a sun started to rise. This was it, exactly what she needed to start over.

"I'll help you finish packing first thing tomorrow, and you can be on your way back to Boston by lunchtime."

She frowned as panic sneaked over her. By lunchtime she'd be gone—forever?

"I can have a cashier's check ready for you first thing tomorrow."

"I... I..."

"In fact, let me call my banker now. Why wait? I'm sure you're anxious to get back to your life and friends." Naldo balled up his linen napkin and rose to his feet.

"But wait—"

"I'll call my lawyer and have him draw up the paperwork."

He was already halfway across the room, cell phone pulled from his pocket, their elegant dinner forgotten in his haste to...

Get rid of her.

Irritation shimmered through her. It was so easy for him. He wanted the cottage back. She was a problem, and what did a rich man do with his problems? Throw money at them and make them go away.

Even without an in-depth knowledge of local real estate, she was experienced enough to know that a tiny, unrenovated workman's cottage, landlocked in a big estate, on one grass-covered acre was worth...what? One hundred thousand? If that. And that would be the price of the land. The 1920s cottage, with its pokey rooms and vintage fixtures would be a tear-down to all but the most hardened history buffs.

Why was he willing to pay so much to get rid of her? And why so fast?

Alarm bells jangled her nerves.

"Why did your father leave my mother that cottage?" Her voice sounded calmer than she felt.

Naldo paused in the act of dialing. "She worked here

for fifteen years. She was a loyal and dedicated employee. Giving bequests to valued staff is a family tradition."

"But every other longtime member of staff got a cash gift."

Naldo held her gaze for a moment, then looked away and cleared his throat.

"My father knew the estate was very dear to her, and he wanted to make sure she always had a home here."

"I'm sure most of the staff feel the same way. The estate is famous as a place where people live out their whole lives, even when they're too old to work. That's one of the many traditions that make it such a special—"

A bizarre thought accompanied a rush of ice to her veins.

"Did your father suspect that you might try to get rid of her after his death?"

Naldo's chin lifted just a fraction. Had she imagined it? "Why would I do that? She was the finest cook in central Florida. And, as I said, she was a valued friend." His brows lowered and his eyes narrowed as he crossed his hands over his chest. "Two hundred and fifty thousand."

Anna blinked. Her heart pumped painfully in her chest. What on earth was going on?

Her mom's brief will, prepared on store-bought software, left Anna everything except her savings. And a handwritten note on the printout had made it clear how much it meant to her mother that she really had something precious to leave. The will itself had not spelled out exactly what that was, beyond her personal belongings. Presumably because she hadn't actually inherited until after Robert De Leon's death.

Did her mom mean her to keep the cottage and treasure it as she had?

Two hundred and fifty thousand dollars. Of course she had to take it. She'd be a fool not to.

"If the cottage is mine, I could sleep there tonight, couldn't I?"

One of Naldo's eyebrows lifted. "Why on earth would you want to do that?"

"Oh, I don't know. Sentimental reasons, I guess. I lived there for seven years. It holds a lot of fond memories." Her mind raced, trying to figure out why he wanted to buy her out, and so quickly. Why did it matter so much to him?

And maybe spending one night in her old home would make it easier to say goodbye. She'd left for college without a whiff of nostalgia for the old place, with its noisy window-mounted air conditioners and mice scurrying in the attic. She couldn't wait to get away.

She'd only been back a handful of times, and had tried to convince her mom to move up to Boston, but she wouldn't even consider it.

But now, the thought of packing up what could fit in the van and leaving *forever...*

She swallowed hard. "I'll give you my answer in the morning." She set her fork down on the plate. Her appetite had vanished along with their easy camaraderie.

Disbelief and anger fought plainly on Naldo's handsome face. The very rich didn't have to hide their feelings.

"Let me drive you back to your motel." A dark growl.

"No need." She smiled sweetly. "Everything I brought with me is in my van. It's parked outside. And I have the key to the cottage. Same one I took away to college with me."

"You can't sleep there, it's a mess." He shoved a hand through his thick dark hair, disordering it.

His obvious exasperation gave her a thrill of power. *You can't push everyone around, bud.*

"I don't mind. Some clean sheets on the bed and I'll be quite comfortable. It'll help me get a handle on packing, too."

"I'll come with you."

Damn. He still hadn't found what he was looking for. It wasn't in any of the obvious places, and he'd been tied up with funeral arrangements and estate business. What if she found it first? He wanted her to accept his offer and leave immediately. Certainly before she started sniffing around what the legacy of the cookbook might mean.

Naldo held the door of Anna's horrible old white van open for her. "Did you rent this thing?"

"I bought it. I figured it would be perfect for transporting Mom's things back to Boston." She tossed her gold hair back from her forehead, a shimmer of perspiration sparking highlights on her silky skin.

"See you tomorrow." She looked ready to slam the door on him, but he kept his wrist braced, holding it open.

"I'll come along with you, to see if you need anything."

Suspicion flashed in her eyes, which appeared slate blue in the dusk. She had good reason to be suspicious, but no matter. He was guardian of the De Leon heritage, and if protecting the legacy he'd been entrusted with meant ticking someone off, then he had no problem with it. Even if that someone was a very lovely young woman.

He slammed the door and strode around to the passenger seat. He tugged on the handle and it wouldn't open.

Anna leaned across the cab and rolled down the window manually. "That door's sticky. You have to yank on it or it won't budge. There's no need to come. Really. I'll see you tomorrow."

Her voice had a cool finality about it that irked him. The

desire to be rid of him shone plainly in her face and only deepened his determination to go with her.

He tugged on the door. It swung open with a rusty screech and he climbed in and eased himself reluctantly down onto the torn and grimy upholstery.

"How will you get back to the house if you ride with me?" A tiny frown marred her smooth forehead.

"I love walking at night." He shot her a bold grin.

"You would." Was that a smile fighting her primly held lips?

The dash was scratched and covered in greasy finger marks and the sudden flare of headlights illuminated the chipped windshield. "You drove this rattletrap all the way from Boston?" He couldn't hide the disbelief in his voice.

"It runs like a charm." She turned the key in the ignition, keeping her elegant profile to him. The harsh grinding and spluttering that followed contradicted her assertion.

She tossed her hair and lifted her pretty, pointed chin before turning it again. The engine coughed a few times then shuddered to life with a pained growl. "See?" She flashed a triumphant glance at him.

She reversed out of the parking space by leaning out the window to see by the dim glow of the taillights, and pulled onto the access road to the cottage and the western part of the estate. The van rattled like a high-speed roller coaster on the graveled surface. Naldo gritted his teeth as the engine whined and groaned.

"I don't like that noise. You should get it checked out. I know a great mechanic in town who'll come out here to look at it. Manny Alvarez. I'll give you his number or I'll call him myself if you like." The engine now sounded like it was about to catch fire. "Seriously, be sure to get it checked out before you head back to Boston."

"Sure. Great. Thanks." Her voice rang with insincerity.

Stubborn. He tried not to smile. Anna always had a little hot pepper in her blood. That's what made her such a fun competitor when they were kids.

She was all grown up now. He took another look at the chiseled features illuminated in the reflected headlights. How did that sports-mad tomboy turn into an elegant woman with the strength and beauty of a fine cut diamond?

"Why are you staring at me?" She turned to him, fire flashing in her eyes.

"Sheer admiration." He let a smile sneak across his lips.

"Well, cut it out. You're making me jumpy."

No ring on her finger, he noted with satisfaction. She was over and done with that guy. Though why he should care, he had no idea.

She pulled up in front of the unlit cottage. The van whimpered gratefully as she turned off the engine. Why would she drive such a banged-up piece of junk now that she had money? He shook his head.

Stubborn.

"I'll go open up for you." He held out his hand for the keys.

"It's okay, I can do it." She levered open her door and jumped down.

"I see you still have to do *everything* for yourself."

"Oh, go ahead." She tossed the keys and he caught them. "I see you can still catch." She winked, which caused an unexpected but pleasant sensation in his groin. "I've got to get something out of the back. You go in and turn on the lights."

"Sure." The darkness hid his evil grin. He opened the door, picked his way carefully across the dark kitchen to the fuse box.

And tripped the circuit breaker.

"Turn the lights on," she called.

"I'm trying. The power's out."

He was glad the darkness concealed the gleam of satisfaction that must be shining in his eyes. He didn't want her to have a chance to poke around—until he had.

"Ugh! How annoying."

"The power's been shaky lately; we've had some storms." No lie there. He crossed his arms over his chest. "It'll probably be back on by morning. I'll call the electric company when I get back to the house."

"How come the power was on at the house?"

"Backup generator. It rolls over right away; you don't even know it's gone out." He ran his tongue over the back of his teeth. *Desperate times call for desperate measures.*

"It's all right for some. I guess the poor peasants who work for you just have to stumble around in the dark."

"Yeah." He grinned in the darkness. Her attitude tickled him.

"I wonder if Mom still keeps the candles in the… Yup! Here they are. And the matches are still right here next to this 'antique' gas stove your high and mightiness never saw fit to replace." The flare of a match lit up her features, one eyebrow raised in a challenge.

"You look lovely by candlelight."

"You, too." She flashed a fake smile. "Well, I'd love to entertain you, but I guess the twelve-course meal I was planning will have to wait. You can start walking."

He could think of plenty of things he'd rather be doing. Like, say, feeling his way to the tiny, hot bedroom in the dark and working up a musky sweat between the sheets with this delicious new Anna and her snippy, fiery attitude. If it wasn't for his duty to the family and the estate, he'd be tempted to strike a match in the fire simmering below her pretty surface.

But unfortunately, in the choice between pleasure and duty, duty would have to win out.

"Are you sure you'll be okay? Need a hand changing the sheets?"

She cocked her head, put her hands on her slim hips and stuck her chest out. *Damn, little Anna had a chest.* And a high, full, perky one, too.

Duty could always wait until tomorrow. He licked his lips.

She narrowed her eyes. "Why do I feel like I'm all alone in grandma's cottage with the big, bad wolf?"

He resisted the urge to growl. "Seriously, I could stay overnight if you don't want to be alone here in the dark." He fought a wicked smile.

She chuckled. "No thanks! I know my way around. I used to live here, remember? I'll just go to bed and start cleaning up in the morning when it gets light."

"Okay." Relief crept through his veins. Of course it didn't do much to dim the desire also creeping through them, but that was nothing a workout in the gym and a cool bath couldn't fix. "See you in the morning."

Two hundred and fifty thousand dollars and she hadn't snatched it up? Morning sunlight blasting through the un-curtained bedroom window of the cottage made Anna squint. Had she completely lost her mind?

It was that infuriating Naldo's fault. Something about his cocky arrogance just lit a stick of dynamite under her stubborn streak. Ugh! Why had she let him get to her? She was in serious danger of cutting off her nose to spite her face.

She hadn't tried to change the sheets in the dark, so they were the same ones her mom must have slept in for the last time just a few horribly long days ago. They still smelled like violets and love—and home.

She rested her head on the soft pillow, wishing she could hug her mom the way she could wrap her arms around the soft cotton of the faded floral pillowcase.

Why did you have to die before we got a chance to really reconnect as adults? A sick feeling of regret sneaked through her. On one hand she was glad her mom had died thinking her successful, but on the other she wished she'd just been honest.

She bit back imminent tears and sat up. Took a deep breath. She didn't deserve the luxury of feeling sorry for herself. The A/C hadn't come back on so the power must still be out and she'd better get that seen to so she could pack up and get out of here before Naldo changed his mind about the money.

She stumbled out of bed and eased up the window without the A/C unit blocking it.

The scent of oranges filled her senses as she leaned out into the rich, dewy morning.

Wow.

How had she forgotten that feeling? Like the whole world was ripe with expectation. With the promise of wonderful things just about to happen.

The new grove of trees Robert De Leon had planted near the cottage ten years earlier had grown from shrubby seedlings into majestic full-grown trees. Their arching branches hung with heavy fruit—a rare heirloom orange from Italy called Summer's Shadow.

He'd planted them because her mother loved orange trees and said she'd like to live right in the middle of a grove if she could. The gruff but charming orange magnate had loved that. They'd picked the variety together, right at this time of year—spring—when the shadow of the past year's summer hung in the sun-ripened fruit almost ready for picking.

And now they were both gone.

She sucked in a breath, determined not to let grief overwhelm her again. She went down the stairs, instinctively ducking her head to avoid the low ceiling beam, and headed straight for the circuit breaker.

Yup, it was tripped. Why on earth hadn't she thought of that last night? It wouldn't occur to Naldo to check the breaker because he had hot and cold running servants to do that kind of thing for him, but she should have known better.

She flipped the black switch and the air-conditioning units whirred to life. Phew. The coffeemaker would work, too, and right now she needed coffee like a vampire needed fresh blood.

As the last drips of Colombian Gold splashed down into the pot, she snatched it up and poured herself a steaming mug.

Ahh. With the first sip she could feel her synapses begin to fire. She was just about to drink another life-giving draught, when loud banging on the door made her jump.

"What? Who is it?" she spluttered, still half-awake. She really didn't want to open the door in her pink pajama shorts and cami, but another series of pounding knocks drew her out of her chair.

"Hey, Anna." A deep voice penetrated the wood door.

Naldo. What did he want now?

Should she open the door in her PJs? She ran her fingers through her uncombed hair. Maybe if she just kept quiet he'd think she was out?

But the van was parked right outside.

Gritting her teeth she got up and unlatched the door.

Six foot whatever of Naldo filled the doorframe, blocking out the light. He wore the distinctive uniform of his polo team, a black-and-white shirt and white jodhpurs that skimmed his long, powerful legs before diving into tall black leather boots. "Your van is blocking the road." Impatience burned in his eyes. "You must move it immediately."

Was "please" not in this man's vocabulary?

She headed for the kitchen to retrieve the keys, uncomfortably aware of her flimsy pink sleepwear.

"You should park in the carport." He followed her into the kitchen, an act of intrusion that made her hair stand on end.

"The van won't fit. That carport is sized for a Model-T."

"Then park on the lawn."

"Why don't you just drive on the lawn and go around the van, then?" She turned to him, indignation sparking her temper.

His black brows lowered over flashing dark eyes. "The horse trailers require a level surface. This is the only access road to the polo field and the entire team is waiting. Spectators will be arriving any moment." His voice deepened to a growl.

"At this time of the morning? What is it, eight?"

"Of course. Before it gets hot. Hurry!"

Did he just issue an order? Her blood heated several degrees. His arrogance was unbelievable!

On perverse instinct she reached for her coffee cup, lifted it to her lips and took an invigorating sip.

"What are you waiting for?" He looked at her in disbelief, no doubt appalled that she hadn't leapt into action to do his bidding.

"I'm in the middle of my morning coffee. I don't work for you, in case you'd forgotten." Irritation shimmered in her voice. Let him wait for a change.

Naldo crossed his arms over his chest, obviously taking her challenge as the thrown gauntlet she intended. His black eyes held her gaze just long enough for her heart to start pounding against her ribs, then he let them drift.

Over her unmadeup face, her neck. She swallowed, her coffee cup quivering in her hand.

His menacing, seductive, dark-lashed eyes slid lower. Over the flimsy pink cotton camisole that clung to her braless breasts. Her nipples rose as if on command, pushing against the soft fabric in direct defiance of her own wishes.

The tiniest hint of a smile twitched at the edge of that wide, arrogant and disgustingly sensual mouth.

Anna lifted the cup and took a deep gulp of coffee, which suddenly tasted bitter as poison.

She shifted her bare feet on the linoleum floor, an action that only drew his attention lower. Those dark, invasive pupils drifted insolently down the length of her bare legs.

Her knees weak and her breath coming in short gulps, Anna tossed her uncombed hair and lifted her chin. "Do you mind?"

"Not at all." His rich, velvety voice thickened as he raised his eyes to meet hers.

He took a step forward, and before she knew what was happening he'd grabbed her keys off the table. Rage slicing through her, she slammed down her cup and swiped at them.

Instead of snatching the keys behind his back, Naldo stepped forward, slid a broad, long-fingered hand around her waist...

And crushed his lips over hers in a hot, heavy and unrelenting kiss.

The scent of him—tangy soap, clean skin and raw, unbridled masculinity—disengaged her faculties. His powerful hands held her firm while he feasted on her mouth.

Her lips parted to welcome his tongue as her nipples stung with painful arousal, crushed against his thick chest.

Naldo De Leon is kissing me.

The eager tenth-grader inside her thrilled with the astonishing and unexpected pleasure of a dream come true. A dream cherished and nurtured for so long that it had taken on the weight of a legend.

Her body hummed with trills of delight right to her toes and fingertips. A shock of sizzling chemistry and magic made the proverbial fireworks dance behind her closed eyelids. Her body swayed in his arms as she melted in the searing heat of his kiss.

Then he pulled back. Eyes narrowed, gleaming.

Her heart thumped as her hand flew to her mouth. *What on earth had just happened?*

Naldo held up her keys.

"Thank you." Cool and dismissive, his words echoed in her ears as he turned and strode from the room.

Three

Anna stomped along the sidewalk, chest ready to burst with anger. Naldo De Leon deserved a public flogging. No. Flogging was too good for him. A hanging would be better.

The nerve of him to march right into *her* kitchen and kiss her as if he was an eighteenth-century Duke and she was some comely serving wench he fancied that morning.

Arrrggghhh! She fought the urge to scream out loud in broad daylight in the middle of town. Round Lake was a sleepy, relaxed burg reminiscent of *Mr. Rogers' Neighborhood*. Right now the bright noon sunlight gleaming off neat storefronts and smiling shoppers were an affront to her violent mood.

He'd snatched her keys as if they were his! Didn't bring them back, either. Just parked her van on the grass, and left it there with the keys in the ignition.

Unbelievable.

She'd hunkered inside, boiling with rage, while the distant sound of mallets tapping a ball, horses snorting and the cheers of a gaggle of simpering groupies had continued for most of the morning. Then they'd all streamed back past the cottage in their honking great horse trailers and shiny sports cars, off to the next diversion for the rich and idle.

She'd like to take a polo mallet to Naldo and—

But no. She was bigger than that.

She took in a deep breath as she approached the plate-glass window of the lawyer's office. She reached into her bag for the thick envelope the lawyers had handed her after the will reading.

The deed and map to *her* property.

Her mood was considerably less punchy when she left the office half an hour later, her brain humming with talk of "easements" and "use-by-right" and "right-of-way."

None of which she had. The lawyer had laughed at the idea of going up against the De Leons with a claim of "adverse possession." It would require an expensive legal wrangle with minimal chance of success.

She had no choice but to sell to Naldo.

Once again, she was rattled and ticked off to find him inside the cottage when she returned.

"What are you doing in my mother's house?"

Still in his mud-spattered polo uniform, Naldo filled the tiny kitchen. "Looking for you."

"So you thought you'd just let yourself in and wait?" She crossed her arms over her chest, as her blood temperature rose. "You're getting the floor dirty."

Naldo glanced down at his tall black boots, which weren't nearly as clean as they'd been that morning. "I'll send someone over to tidy up."

"The door was locked."

"I have a key." He flashed his palm, where a key glinted. Not unlike the gleam in his wicked black eyes.

"This is my property now. You have no right!" Her voice rose to a squeak.

She took a deep breath to calm herself. No sense getting all huffy. She needed to sell the property to Naldo, or it was as good as worthless.

Play nice.

"I'm sorry. I'm just a little emotional, I guess. It's been a rough few days."

"I know. I apologize for kissing you this morning. It was inappropriate."

His face was serious, not a glimpse of teasing humor.

He was sorry for kissing her.

A deflating rush of disappointment slackened her muscles. Had she hoped he'd be overcome with passion and longing for more? That he'd fall madly in love with her?

Puh-lease.

"Apology accepted," she said stiffly.

"I've had a tough few days, too. I guess I'm a little strung out."

She nodded, wishing he would just leave while she still had some semblance of control.

His wide, dark eyes held her gaze with gripping intensity. "Would you do me the honor of having dinner with me again tonight? I'm rather ashamed of my behavior, both last night and this morning, and I'd like a chance to make it up to you."

Again, the serious expression. No hint of mockery.

Anna swallowed. *Would you do me the honor?*

His words struck a raw nerve. Naldo talking to her like she was a real person, deserving of respect.

Get over yourself. He just wants to butter you up so he

can buy the land back. And you need to sell it to him as much as he needs to buy it.

"Yes, I'll come."

He nodded, then executed a half bow, like an ancient courtier. "I'll pick you up at seven-thirty."

He left her frowning and trying to ignore an infuriating rush of excitement. *It's only business. Tonight you can exchange the papers for money, and tomorrow you can leave with your dignity intact.*

As the door closed behind him, the footprints on the linoleum drew her attention. They weren't just between the door and the spot where he'd been standing in front of the kitchen sink. They went all around the kitchen, into the tiny bathroom. She traced them. Not really footprints, just hints of dirt here and there.

He's been up the stairs, she noticed with a frisson of alarm. A clod of earth sat on the top step.

Telltale grains and blades of grass revealed that he'd been into her mom's bedroom, and her old one, too. Of course he was far too arrogant to think about making a mess in someone else's house. Used to people cleaning up after him.

But what on earth was he doing up there?

She chewed her knuckle for a moment, trying to make sense of it. Maybe he was trying to reassure himself that it was still his?

Or was he looking for something?

She was primped and zipped into a pale blue dress by the time Naldo's shiny red Alfa Romeo sidled up to her decrepit van that evening.

His expression of grim determination made her stomach curl as she stood at the kitchen window watching him stride up to the front door.

"Hello." She managed a bright smile as she opened it, ready to step outside. Naldo looked over her shoulder into the cottage.

"Been packing, I see."

He looked frighteningly handsome in a pale linen shirt tucked into expensively hip jeans.

"Yes. I got some things boxed up this afternoon. I can't seem to throw anything away. I had no idea my mom kept every issue of *Better Homes and Gardens* since 1997, with Post-it notes marking the recipes she liked. I even found an article where she got the idea for the embroidered curtains upstairs."

She realized she was yammering out of nerves and held her tongue.

"Shall we go?" Naldo extended his hand. Not sure what else to do, she lifted hers. He took it, looked into her eyes for one blistering second, then pressed his lips to her fingers.

Heat flared through her like a struck match.

Gulp.

He dropped her hand and pushed out the door, leaving her blinking and flustered. She should be annoyed at his inappropriately bold behavior, especially after this morning's brash and obnoxious kiss, but somehow...

He opened the passenger door for her and she lowered herself into the racing-style seat. As Naldo climbed into his seat and started the engine, she struggled into the seat belt that reminded her of the harness in a child's car seat.

"I don't think we'll crash between here and the house." Amusement tugged at his mouth. "I guess you're more cautious than when we used to drag race Dad's golf carts."

"With wisdom comes caution." She finally snapped the complicated latch closed over her chest. She felt like she was lying on her back in the low-slung car, a sensation that made her already queasy stomach tighten.

"You used to be up for pretty much anything in the old days."

"I was young and stupid."

"You were fun." The engine growled to life. "We had a lot of good times together." He shot her a black glance loaded with suggestion.

If only.

"Yes. I was one of the guys, wasn't I? Always good for a pickup game or a fourth in tennis." She didn't like the bitterness in her voice.

He raised an eyebrow as he backed onto the drive. "You sound like you wanted more."

I did.

"You once said you'd take me to my prom." She regretted the words the instant they'd left her mouth. His casual comment had meant so much to her. How many hours had she lain in bed and dreamed of walking into the school gym with Naldo on her arm?

"I did?" Naldo looked at her in astonishment.

Her gut clenched. "Such a laughable idea?"

"I'm not laughing. I just don't remember."

She stared at his aristocratic profile as he drove through the orchards. He didn't even *remember* something that had meant the world to her. What a childish delusion to think that the great Naldo De Leon would accompany her to the prom at the local public school, a place he had certainly never set foot in his life.

"Why would you remember? It doesn't mean anything." Again, the edge in her voice made her grit her teeth. Only twenty-six years old and already bitter. She hated that.

"I admit I didn't really see you that way. You were a pal, a buddy, you know."

"Yup. I know. And you're right. We did have a lot of fun together." She looked at him cautiously, and noticed a dimple appear under his cheekbone. She remembered that dimple from the times they'd laughed together. Those times had meant a lot to her, even if they hadn't to him. Her and Naldo, together in Paradise. "In all honesty, those were the best years of my life."

His head whipped around and his intense stare made her wish she could swallow her words. But what did it matter? Tomorrow she'd finish packing and be gone.

They drove to the main house in a silence thick with emotion and unspoken words.

"It's all yours now," she said, as the beautifully proportioned redbrick mansion with its thick white columns and wide verandas came into view. "It's such a lovely house. Is it really four hundred years old?"

Naldo laughed. "No way. I don't even know how many times my ancestors rebuilt, what with hurricanes and forest fires and you name it. This one's been here since 1912. The exterior walls are two feet thick."

"Why so massive?"

"Can't be blown down, can't burn down." He shot her a dimpled grin. "Since the family has always been dead set against insurance, they like to make their investments indestructible."

"It's not insured?"

"Nope. The De Leons have always been too proud to take anyone else's money, and we don't give it away on the off chance of disaster, either. My dad always called it 'betting against success.'"

"I guess the De Leons have always had so much money they can handle a setback without going under."

"Exactly." He pulled the car up in front of the house. "Let me help you with that." He leaned over and unlatched the harness keeping her pinned in the severely reclined seat. His long, strong fingers brushed her breasts as he removed the straps, sparking shimmers of heat that she tried her best to ignore. She struggled out of the race car with as much dignity as she could muster. Her heels sank into the thick gravel as they walked toward the grand front entrance.

"You look beautiful." A dark note of approval thickened Naldo's voice.

"Thanks." She tucked a strand of hair behind her ear. He took her arm as they walked up the wide stone steps to the doors. She had the eerie sensation of a dream coming true, but too late, and all wrong.

He'd been gorgeous as a boy, all lanky grace and teasing humor. Now taller, with the muscled build of a keen athlete and the languid poise of a man fully aware of his own power, he was breathtaking. His sharp cheekbones and strong jawline contrasted intriguingly with the easy charm of his dimpled smile and flashing black eyes.

Oh, Naldo. It was a good thing she'd been up in Boston for the last eight years, not down here pining over a man she could never have.

The double doors opened as if by magic.

"Thanks, Pilar." He smiled at the housekeeper.

Anna mumbled "Hi," feeling as if she were on the wrong side of the master/servant divide.

Naldo still held her arm in his, and she could feel the warmth of his skin through the fine linen of his shirt. Her body tingled with awareness of his masculine presence. A flashback to the lightning intensity of his kiss made her nipples sting. The sensation of arousal was undercut by a sharp pang of regret that he'd never hold her in his arms again.

Are you nuts? This man was arrogant enough to kiss you without permission and now you're thinking about—

"It looks like dinner's ready." This time he guided her into the grand dining room where two places were set opposite each other at the end of the polished mahogany table.

"Your dad always liked to eat in here. Are you going to continue the tradition?" *Or is this just set up to intimidate me?*

Each place held three crystal glasses and at least twelve pieces of solid silver cutlery. Priceless porcelain plates displayed an arrangement of miniature garden vegetables.

"Traditions can be reassuring at a time of change." She felt a tiny chill of loss as he slid his arm out of hers to pull back her chair.

She looked up at the large oil portrait hanging over the marble fireplace. "That's a lovely portrait of your mother. She was very beautiful."

The supercilious black-haired beauty glared down at her, shimmering in a crisply painted black silk evening gown that swept around her elegant figure. Anna remembered her as a chilly, quick-tempered woman with a critique for everything and everyone poised on the tip of her tongue.

"She was brilliant, too. She spoke seven languages and was an accomplished dancer before she married my father."

"I remember that room upstairs with the barre and the wall of mirrors. Was that hers?" She hadn't known it was there until after his mother died. It was off-limits before that.

"Yes, she had to dance every day or her muscles ached. She could have been a prima ballerina."

"Why did she stop?"

"Can you picture my father allowing his wife to dance on stage?" Naldo raised an eyebrow as he took a sip of white wine.

"Ballet? It's hardly the Moulin Rouge."

"She knew her role when she married. To stand by his side at the head of the estate, to bear an heir. To love her husband."

A dark undertone in his voice surprised her. The De Leons always looked like the perfect couple: both clever, striking, rich, dripping with style. Had it been a facade?

"Did your parents have a happy marriage?" Since her divorce she had a sharp curiosity about other people's marriages. Why did some loves last a lifetime and others…turn out not to have been love at all?

"Of course they had a good marriage. A great marriage." Naldo's brusque reply made her regret her blunt question.

"I confess I was always a little afraid of your mom. She was so…perfect."

"She was a perfectionist. So am I. If something's worth doing, it's worth doing right. I'm sure you agree."

"Absolutely. Speaking of which…" She looked at the array of cutlery surrounding her plate as a flush rose to her cheekbones. "Which one do I use?"

"You start from the outside and work your way in. Or at least that's what you're supposed to do. You can go ahead and use the dessert spoon if you like. It won't bother me." He speared a baby carrot and crunched it.

She smiled and picked up the outside fork.

Naldo leaned back in his chair, glad the potentially dangerous subject of his mother and his parents' marriage had been deftly swept aside. For an intense second he'd experienced an irrational temptation to tell her the truth.

But propriety won out, as it always did. He'd been brought up to protect the family honor at all costs.

That meant keeping its secrets.

As Anna speared a piece of cauliflower and placed it carefully between those plump pink lips, thoughts of secrets sank into a warm flood of desire.

He couldn't take his eyes off her. Her girlish features had matured into refined feminine beauty. Her liquid blue eyes held shadowed depths that suggested wisdom beyond her years and a few intriguing secrets of her own. The slender physique showcased by her elegant powder-blue dress expressed its power in subtle strength rather than raw muscularity.

But nothing compared with the vision of her that morning. In her clinging pink PJs, golden hair mussed from sleep, cheeks rosy with indignation—

He took another sip of wine. Anna looked especially beautiful when she was a little hot and bothered and he couldn't help wanting to see her in that delightful condition again.

Would it be so wrong to have a little fun before they conducted their business? The attraction was mutual, no question about it. She'd melted into his kiss like liquid fire. The chemistry leaping between them was explosive.

If she made love anything like she played tennis...

"Naldo." Pilar's voice snapped him out of his reverie and drew his attention to the doorway. "Isabela is here. She said she'd be right in for dinner."

Naldo frowned. "I thought she was dining in St. Augustine tonight."

Pilar shrugged. "I told Vicki to cook another filet. Shall I lay a third place?"

"Yes, please do."

Damn. His sister's arrival put a wrinkle in his impromptu plans to seduce Anna tonight. He'd secretly hoped Isabela would return to Paris immediately, the way she usually did after her perfunctory visits to the old homestead. But he didn't want her to feel she was no longer welcome here now the house was his. He was head of the family now and it was his duty to keep it together.

"Isabela." He rose to his feet as his sister swept into the room with a flutter of chiffon. "Please join us. Do you know Anna Marcus?"

That halted big sis in her tracks. She looked at Anna, who'd risen to her feet in expectation of a polite greeting. Those sharp black eyes met Anna's blue ones and a tiny wrinkle appeared in his sister's smooth, pale brow.

The two women sized each other up for a tense moment, then Isabela came forward, heels clicking on the parquet. "I don't believe we've met."

"No, I guess not." Anna shook her hand and smiled. "I think you were studying in Europe by the time I moved here with my mom. You live there now, don't you?"

"Paris. Except when I travel for my work." Isabela swished past Anna to the end of the table, where a third place was laid.

"Isabela is an opera director." Naldo sat down and replaced his napkin with a flourish. "She prefers art and life on the continent."

"There are a lot of wonderful opera companies in the States, too, aren't there?" Anna said brightly.

Isabela gave her a withering look. "They hardly compare to the Paris Opera and La Scala. Ugh, these vegetables are positively wilted." She picked at a miniature spear of broccoli with her fork. "Europe certainly has better-trained staff." She poked at an ornamental curl of carrot, then looked up. "Oh, sorry, no offense intended. I forgot for a moment that your mother was a member of the staff."

"Yes. She cooked here for fifteen years." Anna beamed with convincing pride that gave Naldo a warm glow. Not many women could go toe-to-toe with Isabela De Leon.

"I know. I saw you at the will reading. Rather an impressive legacy for a cook, wouldn't you say?" Isabela took a sip of wine, leaving a neat semicircle of plum lipstick on the rim.

"I guess your father knew how much my mom loved her home here."

"Or was it because she was such a *treasured friend?*"

Naldo's spine stiffened. *What was his sister up to now?* She was as dangerous and unpredictable as that enormous poodle she used to take everywhere with her. "Isabela's a free spirit. She never stays in one place for long. When are you heading back to Paris?"

"I thought I might stay a while." Isabela tilted her head. Her hair stayed lacquered to her perfectly shaped skull. "Paris can be so crowded at this time of year. Life would be much more bearable if I had a little place to get away from it all."

"You do. Your house in the Cap D'Antibes, remember? Not to mention your villa on Lake Como."

"Ugh, those places are simply mobbed with frightful tourists. I can hardly bear to set foot in them. I think something more rustic, an estate in the Loire Valley, perhaps. Somewhere like this place where I can commune with nature and grow things."

Naldo didn't even try to suppress the hearty chuckle that bubbled to his throat. "Grow things? I've never known you to have an interest in growing anything except your fingernails."

"I'm maturing, darling. And as an artist I have a height-ened appreciation for the beauty of nature. Do you remember Mother's dream of buying a bit of land and moving the family back to Europe?"

"Mother's dream didn't have anything do with growing things. She just never felt at home here in the States."

"Exactly, darling! And all this sweating and grunting over a bunch of oranges is so undignified. Just think how much better you'd live in France. You could own a vineyard and make champagne. You could use the family title again. I could hold my head up in society. I can't even stand to drink orange juice. It gives me indigestion."

"There are a lot more people in the world drinking orange juice than there are drinking champagne."

"A perfect reason to stick with champagne." Isabela lowered her thick lashes over her dark eyes.

"I'm sure we're boring Anna with this family chitchat." Naldo leaned back in his chair. "I invited her here tonight to discuss an agreement over the land."

"I hardly see why one acre makes any difference one way or the other." Isabela took a sip of her wine. "If you had any sense you'd carve the whole thing up into a subdivision. With all those snowbirds looking for a piece of Florida sunshine, the real estate market is booming."

Irritation flared in his gut. "You know I'll never sell."

"No? We'll see."

Anna's gaze jumped from him to Isabela like someone watching a tennis match. Her obvious intelligence was on high alert. At the awkward lull in the conversation, she frowned. "I can kind of see why your father left my mother the land, but what did he mean by the cookbook?"

"She was the cook, wasn't she?" Isabela didn't bother to look at her as she picked up an asparagus stalk between two long fingers and crunched it.

"Well, yes, but I don't know what book he was talking about. I found a few cookbooks in the cottage, and mom kept her favorites in the kitchen here at the house, but do you know which one he meant?"

Naldo shifted in his chair and cleared his throat. That was a whole different can of worms he'd rather not open at all. With Letty gone and business-minded Anna in her place, it could prove to be complicated and expensive in ways his father had never intended.

"Who knows?" Isabela mopped up some dip with a tiny celery stalk. "Daddy was obviously going soft in the head. Why in Heaven's name would he care about a cookbook? What he should have done was divide the estate equally between his two children instead of following some disgusting, outdated and sexist tradition."

Naldo resisted the urge to growl with exasperation. "You receive enough money every month to live like a queen. You know the De Leon family is where we are today exactly because we have never veered from the path of tradition. How many other families can claim more than four hundred years of stewardship on the same property?"

"In Europe, plenty. If the family was based there, perhaps I'd be able to live with a little dignity."

"Dignity would be about all we'd have left after European estate taxes." Naldo took a bite of asparagus.

"What rubbish. You're rich as Croesus, you just don't want to share with your own flesh and blood. Tradition be damned."

Naldo held her cold gaze. "Tradition is the lifeblood of this family."

Isabela stared back. "Tradition." She drew the word out, and her plum lips widened into a mocking smile. "I suppose that explains this intimate dinner I interrupted."

"Anna and I are old friends. I'm delighted to renew our acquaintance."

What was Isabela up to? He didn't want to think about her. Right now he'd like to ditch this spoiled dinner and acquaint himself with the feel of Anna's lithe body on fresh cotton sheets. He knew her lips tasted like ripe strawberries, but what did the nape of her neck taste like? And those eager nipples?

As he pondered these intriguing questions, Anna's eyes narrowed in a way that did dangerous things to his libido.

"How sweet, but aren't you worried about stirring up old rumors, darling?" Isabela swirled wine around in her glass. "I'm sure tongues are already wagging after the will reading, though I suppose it hardly matters. Everyone from here to Palm Beach knows about Daddy's little affair."

Naldo clenched his fists. "Your flair for the dramatic is impressive." He glanced at Anna, who was busy eating and showed no sign of comprehension, thank goodness. "We both know our father chose to honor Mother's memory by staying single after her death."

"He hardly had any choice, under the circumstances." Isabela's eyes narrowed and Naldo wondered for a single grim instant if she was going to reveal the truth about their mother's death.

Something the family had vowed *never* to speak of.

The silence throbbed with tension.

"Relax, Naldo." Isabela ran a fingertip around the rim of her wineglass, sending a squeal into the thick air. "All I mean is that men will be men. But even in this charmingly egalitarian nation, one would hardly expect a De Leon to marry his own *cook*."

"What?" Anna looked up.

"Ignore her."

Anna stared at Isabela. "Are you saying that your father…and my mother?"

"Don't listen to foolish gossip," Naldo hissed.

Isabela laughed, an ugly sound like breaking glass. "Oh, Naldo. Only men like you and Father would think they could keep an affair secret for years. After all, what do other people's thoughts and feelings matter when you are the lord and master of all you survey?" She tossed her napkin onto the table. "All this warm family reminiscing is giving me indigestion. I'll take supper in my room."

He clenched his fists harder as she rose from her chair and sashayed out of the room.

"Naldo." Anna's voice was a whisper. "It's true, isn't it?"

"Nonsense." He drained his wineglass. Grabbed the bottle and poured another glassful. Knocked it back.

"But it makes perfect sense. That he would leave her the land…" Anna gripped the table, her knuckles white.

Naldo still couldn't believe his father had committed that final act of betrayal after the devastation his affair had already caused the family. The long liaison had been a brittle bone of contention between them. Never discussed, never resolved. A burr in their close and loving relationship that he'd always hoped would go away.

And now it never would because he was dead.

Naldo leaned back into his chair.

"I can see from your face that it's true." Anna lowered herself back into her chair. Those wide blue eyes tore into him like a laser. "I know you don't want it to be, but it makes too much sense."

"You're right. I wish it wasn't true." He leaned forward and planted his elbows on the table, raw pain searing through him. Anger at the wrongs that would now never be righted. "It's your mother's fault that my father is dead."

Four

"What?" Anna blinked. Cold disbelief at all she'd just heard warred with rising indignation.

"Her death killed him." His eyes looked hollow.

"She died in an accident. How could it be her fault?"

Naldo stared at her for a moment, his face stony. "When my father got the phone call that your mother had been in a car wreck, I drove him to the hospital. By the time we arrived she was already in the morgue. When he saw her there…"

Anna froze at the image of her mother laid out in a hospital morgue.

Naldo took a deep breath. "He collapsed. I caught him as he fell, and they revived him right away." His eyes narrowed. "But he never recovered consciousness. It was a massive heart attack. They kept him alive for three days, hooked up to machines, with wires all over his body. And then he was gone."

Anna bit her lip hard. "He died of a broken heart," she whispered.

Naldo's black eyes seemed to look right through her. "He's gone. That's all I know."

"I can't believe she never told me."

They'd been so close.

At least she thought they had. Of course she'd left home eight years ago to go to college, and hadn't had the money, then the time, to come back for more than a handful of brief visits.

The charged atmosphere was interrupted by the arrival of the smiling new cook bearing two plates heaped with fragrant food. Fresh agony streamed through Anna at the memory of her mother doing just that. The cook stopped, perhaps caught off guard by Anna's stricken face.

"Filet of sole in a dill sauce, with new potatoes and a medley of seasonal—"

"Thank you, Vicki. It looks delicious." Naldo cut off her increasingly quavering announcement.

Vicki, who was young, plump and pretty, placed the plates in front of them and shot a sympathetic glance at Anna.

She tried to smile back.

When Vicki left, closing the door discreetly behind her, Anna stared at Naldo. "She never said anything. I had no idea."

"Perhaps she knew it was *wrong*." He stabbed his fish with a silver fork.

"But why wrong? Your father was a widower. She wasn't ever married. They were both consenting adults. Middle-aged ones, at that."

"My father made a commitment to my mother." His mouth set in a grim line.

Anna expelled an exasperated breath. "Marriage is

'until death do us part.' I don't doubt that he loved your mother with all his heart, but that doesn't mean he had to die along with her. Didn't you want him to be happy?"

"He was happy." His intense stare pricked her skin.

"Yes." She inhaled slowly. "Apparently he was happy with my mother." It infuriated her that Naldo had planned to keep the whole affair a secret from her. What else was he keeping secret? "Is that why you were snooping around the house this morning? Were you looking for evidence to destroy?"

A frown line appeared between Naldo's brows.

"You left footprints all over the house. Upstairs."

He studied her for a moment, then sat back in his chair. "I was looking for something, yes."

"What?"

"Some jewelry. Family heirlooms that my father gave to your mother."

A cold sensation crept up her spine. "He gave my mom gifts and you thought you'd just take them back?"

"All of them have been in the family more than a century. They are part of the family legacy. They should be restored to the estate."

"Are they worth a lot?"

"Yes. Naturally I intend to compensate you for their full value."

"Oh, do you?" She didn't believe him for a second. "If you meant to pay, why not just ask for them?"

"Because then you would wonder how they came to be in your mother's possession."

"And you didn't want me to find out about your father's relationship with my mom." She frowned. "He must have truly loved her if he gave her a lot of valuable jewels." A funny feeling in the pit of her stomach accompanied a sudden image of the brusque and lordly Robert De Leon and her funny, gentle mother.

How much fun they'd had choosing those trees for the grove by the cottage. Why had it never occurred to her before that they were intimate?

"It was a relationship of *convenience*, nothing more." Naldo crossed his arms over his chest.

Irritation stiffened her spine. "I see it clearly now. *You* are the reason your father left the land and the cottage to my mom. He knew you hated their relationship, and that you wouldn't want her here to remind you of it. He figured that when something happened to him, you'd make her leave—just like you're trying to get rid of me." Her voice shook on the last words. "Your father didn't want my mom to be forced out of the home she loved."

"She could have bought a much nicer home with the money."

"Two hundred and fifty thousand dollars doesn't go too far these days."

Naldo's eyes simmered with an emotion she couldn't quite read. "All right. Four hundred thousand dollars."

Ice trickled through her veins as she saw the determination in the set of his jaw. He wanted to be rid of her that badly? "Does that include the cost of the jewels?" Her voice sounded as cold and hard as a faceted diamond.

"The jewels can be valued and the price negotiated."

"But you haven't found them yet. Perhaps my mom sold them already."

"She wouldn't do that."

"No? You don't seem to think much of her, so what makes you think she'd cherish them rather than sell them for cash?"

The door opened and Tom came in to remove the plates.

They'd barely touched their food. Dinner with Naldo didn't encourage an appetite.

A tense silence accompanied Vicki's appearance with two plates of a fresh fruit torte with whipped cream. The family had always liked the cook to serve the food herself so they could admire her presentation and inquire about ingredients and technique. They enjoyed close and warm communication with everyone who worked there. Now, though, Naldo said nothing beyond a polite thanks.

"The staff must have all known," Anna said once Vicki was gone.

"Perhaps."

"And Isabela. It's not quite the secret you hoped."

Naldo turned and looked up at the portrait on the wall. Anna's eyes followed his, and the cool beauty in the painting seemed almost to raise an eyebrow at her in challenge.

"I'm sure I can count on your discretion." Naldo narrowed his eyes as he looked back at Anna. "Neither of us wants our parents to be the subject of prurient gossip."

"Oh, really? Perhaps your father gave my mom those jewels to buy her silence. Paid her to be invisible, a nobody. A secret mistress." She rose to her feet, heart pounding, and threw her napkin on the table next to her untouched dessert. "Well, I'm ashamed to know any of you. My mother was a wonderful loving woman who was treated shamefully by my father and apparently by yours, too."

"You don't understand the situation." Naldo's icy voice chilled her.

"I understand all I need to. My mother was good enough to sleep with, but not good enough to marry." Tears threatened, and she gulped air trying to keep them at bay. It wasn't fair that men could use women and take what they wanted without making any promises in return. Why did women let them get away with it?

Fists clenched against the onslaught of all she'd learned and couldn't even begin to process, she rushed from the dining room. She strode past a startled Pilar, tugged open the heavy front door and flew down the stone steps.

Her van was back at the cottage.

Her heels would be ruined by the time she got home, but she'd have to walk.

Naldo didn't come after her. She'd hardly expect him to. He knew she'd be back for her money.

She knew it, too. And that only made the long, dusty moonlit walk back to the cottage more grueling than ever.

Naldo stood at his bedroom window looking out over the dark shadows of the groves in the predawn hours. Why couldn't Anna just make this easy?

A light shone in the distant upstairs window of the cottage, and his groin stirred as he watched her stretch, as sleepless and restless as himself.

She would sell. There was nothing to keep her here. It was simply a matter of agreeing on the price. What difference did it make that their parents had been lovers? That was in the past and had no bearing whatsoever on the business between them.

Anna lifted her hair off her neck. Though he was too far away to see details, he had a flash of insight into exactly how that action would stretch her flimsy T-shirt over those high, firm, full breasts.

He wheeled away from the window, desire thickening inside him. It struck him as ironic that his father probably stood at that same window looking out at his own lover.

His chest tightened. His father had been a good man. A

caring and affectionate man. And he'd loved Letty Marcus like a wife.

Was it fair for him to let Anna think he'd merely used her? His barbed remark at dinner—that theirs was nothing but a relationship of convenience—dishonored his father's memory as well as her mother's, and left a bitter taste in his mouth.

He ran a hand through his hair, then stretched to try and release the tension in his shoulders.

Anna's tearful departure left him unsettled, edgy. They'd both feel better if he soothed her and calmed her so she could get some sleep. He'd smooth her ruffled feathers, then they could get back on course and get this deal resolved.

His impulse to visit her in the dead of night had absolutely nothing to do with him wanting to kiss that exasperating mouth into breathless silence and plumb its warm depths with his tongue. He had no thoughts whatsoever of peeling the clothes off that lithe, athletic body and investigating its warm, musk-scented mysteries.

Quite the opposite.

The night air would cool his blood.

It was 3:00 a.m. and Anna had torn the cottage apart looking for the jewels. She'd even slit open the undersides of the mattresses. The cottage was so small there just weren't that many hiding places to check.

The shocking knowledge of her mother's affair with Robert De Leon made her see every object and slip of paper in the cottage in a new light. Would she stumble across love notes? Secret tokens? After six hours of rifling through drawers and even through boxes she'd already packed, she found nothing. Her mother had been absolutely discreet.

Somehow that made her sadder than ever. So loyal to her beloved boss—and lover—that she'd never dared mention her relationship with him to her own daughter. The jewels were probably locked in a safe in the big house. Her mom would hardly have worn them out in public, and Naldo was right, she'd never have sold them.

She rubbed her tired eyes with her hands. Her mother's mysteries were destined to remain just that. A life of quietly kept secrets. Like the identity of Anna's father, a man who'd gotten her mom pregnant, then casually revealed that he was already married.

Anna reflected that she had good reason to hate all men and their cruel games. She'd married Barry Lennox five years ago, filled with hope for a long and happy life together, and he'd betrayed her in every possible way.

Marriage had meant everything to her. A pledge to care for each other, the promise of a lifetime commitment, the assurance that they were equal partners in a relationship. She'd always promised herself she'd never settle for less, that she'd never make the same mistakes her mother did and let a man use her, but he'd done it anyway.

She sank into the old sofa, hearing the springs creak like they did when she was ten and she and her mom had arrived here from Cincinnati to start a new life.

Fresh tears pricked the backs of her eyelids. Could she find enough hope to start all over...*again?*

A sharp rap on the door made her catch her breath.

"Anna."

What the heck is Naldo doing here at three in the morning?

"I know you're up. I saw you moving."

"Go away." She couldn't hide the tears in her voice.

"Let me in, please."

"You've got the key," she muttered.

She gritted her teeth as she heard him use it. Wiping her eyes, she rose to her feet as Naldo appeared in the doorway.

His hair was uncombed and dipping into his eyes, which fixed on hers in the dim light. With his fine linen shirt wrinkled and untucked, he didn't look nearly as elegant and imposing as he had earlier.

Unfortunately he didn't look any less breathtakingly handsome.

She attempted to summon a fresh nugget of hatred for him, but found she didn't have the strength.

"I saw your light on. I can't sleep, either." His voice was low.

"I was looking for the jewels. They're not here." She tried to sound cold, but just sounded tired.

"Never mind about the jewels." He took a step toward her. The overhead light glazed his features as he moved under it. "Your mother made my father happy. He did love her. He loved her very much."

His words, and the strange look in his eyes, made her catch her breath. "Why are you telling me this?"

But Naldo didn't speak. He stepped forward and took her in his arms. Somewhere in the back of her mind she tried to conjure a protest, but it withered as his strong, warm arms closed around her.

His sturdy embrace undermined the last of her carefully guarded strength. She'd had no arms to rest in for so long.

"I hadn't been back to visit in nearly three years." The horrible confession underscored how much she'd lost. Her heart ached.

"She knew you cared. That you were working hard." His powerful fingers moved over her back, stroking her skin through her T-shirt. The caring gesture made her heart beat faster.

"I'm so sorry about your father, Naldo. I know you were very close."

"There'll never be anyone like him." The sadness in his voice made her stomach clench.

"You're like him."

"Yeah. Stubborn as a mule and twice as tough. I probably should have been in the library reading condolences this afternoon, but I was out in the groves checking the irrigation just like my dad would have been." His chest shook with a deep, silent laugh.

She opened her eyes. "Don't you have employees to do that for you?"

"Of course." A twinkle of humor shone in his serious dark eyes. "But we do it because the trees are family to us. The land is in our blood. Sand and grit."

A warm chuckle rose inside her. "Especially the grit. You always did have plenty of that."

"You, too." He rubbed her back again and her fingertips sank into the soft linen of his shirt. Hard muscle matched his hard-nosed attitude. "We're both tough and stubborn and that's why we'll get on with our lives and make them both proud."

You will, but will I? She couldn't be sure of anything anymore. Her brash youthful confidence had been beaten to its knees by betrayal, divorce, bankruptcy and now the loss of the one person in the world she could always count on to be there for her. It would take every last ounce of grit to start over.

She realized Naldo was staring at her. The heat of his gaze threatened to sear right through her skin. For a second she was conscious of her tearstained appearance, then her thoughts seemed to slip sideways and the hot, musky male scent of him crept over her.

His lips were on hers before she could summon a protest. His warm tongue slid into her mouth, gathering hers as he hugged her into his embrace. Reassuring, strengthening, the power of his arms filled her with sensations she hadn't dared to crave.

Desire rippled through her like gasoline on water, threatening to ignite. His hands roamed over her back, and lower, reaching boldly into her shorts to cup her buttocks.

She groaned as he sucked her lower lip and trailed kisses over her cheek. Her fingertips dug into the thick muscle of his back before rising to tangle themselves in his silky hair, then sliding down to rove over the rough denim of his jeans.

A deep, masculine groan emerged as she slid her fingers inside his waistband. She felt him harden against her, straining against the zipper of his jeans. A high note of pure, quivering arousal shot through her.

How much she'd once craved this moment. She and Naldo, wrapped together.

His tongue pushed between her lips, stealing her breath. She rubbed her breasts against his chest, her nipples craving contact with the hard muscle as her hips pushed into his.

I love you, Naldo. I always have.

The stray thought startled her and she pushed it aside. But she didn't push aside the hands that reached under her T-shirt, unfastened her bra and lifted the flimsy shirt over her head.

Naldo's lips parted as he lifted her bra straps off her shoulders, releasing her breasts. He cupped one in his broad hand and the roughness of his callused palm surprised her as he grazed her nipple, sparking a shiver of arousal.

With a swift movement that made her gasp, he gathered her in his arms and sat her unceremoniously on top of the Formica kitchen table she'd once done her homework at.

The cool, smooth surface, with its metal edge, made her aware of the aroused wetness of her sex inside her thin cotton shorts.

His eyes slid shut as he lowered his mouth over her nipple with a low groan. Eyes open in wonder, brain clouded with delicious arousal, she played in his hair with her fingers as he buried his dark head at her breast.

He sucked hard, and her pulse and breathing quickened. She squirmed on the table. Naldo dove lower, mouthing her belly, running his big hands over her thighs.

The sensations he triggered inside her felt so good. Pure pleasure, flowing over her skin and along her limbs. A feeling of being treasured, cared for, *loved.*

He doesn't love you. The thought stabbed her like a shard of memory.

A relationship of convenience. How he'd described the match between his father and her mother.

He was lonely, she was here.

At that moment he tugged at her shorts and panties and dove inside, pushing his face to her crotch. His tongue tickled her aroused flesh as he explored the moist heat. He sucked hungrily, his hands now pressed into her thighs, pushing them against the metal table edge.

An intense expression contorted his handsome features. His eyes squeezed shut, his hair hanging damp on his forehead, he looked totally absorbed.

In her.

She shuddered as his tongue flicked over her sensitive flesh, overwhelmed by sensations that jumbled her thoughts and shook her to the core.

Naldo pulled back and his eyes met hers. His dark gaze, serious, penetrating—demanding—called to something deep inside her.

Wordless, he wrapped his arms around her and lifted her gently off the table. He cradled her as he carried her up the narrow staircase into the bedroom where she'd slept last night.

He lowered her carefully onto the bed and she pulled him to her. She tugged his buttons through the holes in the soft linen, reaching for the warm skin beneath, then shoved his shirt back over his shoulders as the soothing weight of his chest sank into her.

His teeth grazed her neck, then he layered soft kisses over her cheeks and onto her parted lips. He didn't stop kissing, the pressure more urgent, as he fumbled with his zipper and shoved his jeans down.

Excitement built inside her as she helped him ease the stiff fabric over his powerful thighs. He had to pull back to step out of his jeans, and the shock of cool air on her face and chest made her open her eyes. The sight of Naldo—naked—made her catch her breath.

Thick muscle, tan skin accented with sworls of black hair, that arrogant, handsome face—everything about him was riveting male perfection.

His expression focused, he eased her shorts and panties off. Without missing a beat, he pulled a condom seemingly out of thin air and rolled it on. Her belly quivered at the sight of him, hard and eager, yet controlled.

With his thumb and finger he lifted her chin and raised her face to his scorching black gaze.

"Anna," was all he said before he caught her mouth in a kiss and lowered his big body onto hers.

Slow, restrained and quivering with arousal, he slid deep inside her. She writhed, unable to control a moan of intense pleasure as he filled her.

The delicious masculine weight of him pinned her to the

soft mattress. Raw excitement surged through her and she wriggled under him, wanting to be free, and not wanting to be free at all.

Naldo's low groans and heady male scent filled her senses. His hands cupped her face and he kissed her, softly, on the lips, then harder, forceful, as he pushed into her.

She raised her hips to his, jousting with him, pushing into him and drawing back, teasing and tantalizing, building a rhythm that pounded through them both with feverish intensity.

She wrapped her arms tight around his back and gripped him, as unfamiliar emotions and sensations spiked inside her. She sensed her climax coming—a stark, loaded calm like the tide drawing far out to sea before a tsunami—before it exploded over her as his name flew from her mouth.

"Naldo." The single word pierced the predawn silence as Naldo let out a shout and joined her in a fierce climax of his own.

They lay there locked together, panting, sweat mingling. Naldo's hard-edged cheek on hers, his hands cupping her face, fingers tangled into her hair. His big, heavy body trapped her in a prison of pleasure as he throbbed inside her.

Skin to skin, his heart beating fast and hard against hers, they held each other tight.

It felt so right.

The culmination of a million childish fantasies with nothing childish about it. A haunting, sleep-stealing dream come true.

She and Naldo in each other's arms.

His face nuzzled hers, long black lashes still closed over those intense dark eyes. His breath, warm and sweet on her skin, seemed to breathe new life into her and she felt stronger than she had in months. Years.

Ever.

Naldo shifted to one side and eased his weight off her. A smile slid across his sensual mouth as he kissed her cheek. With one broad hand he eased them both onto their sides, still inside her, and held her close.

His thumb brushed a stray lock of hair off her cheek. The thick lashes lifted and the look he gave her—naked admiration—made her face heat.

"Love all," he murmured.

Her breath caught in her throat. Love? What was he talking about? Her pulse picked up speed. "What?" she managed to ask.

"Tennis. The way you played it—fierce, wild yet controlled. Every game a fight to the death." A dimple appeared beside his wicked smile. "Your passion isn't reserved for the courts."

She stared at him for a moment. He meant "love," as in tennis scoring, not the pledge-my-heart-for-all-time kind.

A shard of disappointment undercut her relief. "I haven't played in a while."

One black eyebrow lifted.

"Tennis, I mean," she blurted.

"Ah." His eyes twinkled. He knew exactly what she meant. "But something tells me you're still on top of your game. Maybe we'll have a chance to play again before you go?" He turned away to remove the condom.

Before you go. His words stung her. A reminder that this heavenly intimacy was very temporary. Probably the only reason he'd allowed it to happen was because he knew she'd soon be far away. No danger of her making pathetic assumptions about any kind of future between them.

"What's the matter?" He settled back into bed, a line between his dark brows.

"Nothing. I'm just tired."

"Then sleep. I'm tired, too." He laid his head on the pillow next to hers, his black hair and tan skin a rich contrast to the pale floral pillowcase.

His long fingers stroked a strand of hair from her face before settling at her waist. Relaxed and comfortable, as if they'd done this a hundred times.

As if they were a real couple.

She closed her eyes, not wanting to be taunted by the blissful vision of Naldo sharing a bed with her. It felt good, she couldn't deny it. She'd been through the wringer lately, so what harm could come of enjoying one night that seemed like a dream?

Naldo's big arm weighed her down with soothing pressure, and she soon found herself floating in a sea of bliss. Her body hummed with sensation, a blend of erotic pleasure and warm relaxation, as she drifted into much-needed sleep.

In the morning, a dent in the pillow was the only sign of Naldo. Anna blinked against the harsh sunlight pouring between the open curtains. Was it a dream?

No. The scent of him lingered on the pillow and she pressed her face into it, enjoying the heady male fragrance.

He must have left early. Probably had estate business to attend to. If he left a note it would likely be downstairs, on the heart-shaped phone pad. But then Naldo was hardly the note-leaving type.

She exhaled, traces of pleasure mingling with trickles of apprehension. What would happen next? Would they get together again?

A scratching sound made her glance up at the old plaster ceiling. They never had been able to get rid of those damn mice, but she couldn't begrudge them their perch on this lovely morning.

A harsh scrape overhead made her start. Mice couldn't make a sound that loud. She sat up in bed. Where on earth were her clothes?

She found her shorts on the floor beside the bed, and scrambled into her old room for a clean T-shirt. As she stood on the landing at the top of the stairs, another sound, like a piece of furniture being dragged, chilled her blood.

"Hey!" The aggressive sound of her voice hid her fear. The scraping stopped. "What's going on up there?" Were there workers on the roof?

She shrieked as a hatch lifted almost directly over her head.

Naldo's head appeared in the black square. "I found the jewels."

Five

"How the hell did you get up there?" Anna's heart pounded.

"Pulled up with my arms. Here, take this." Naldo lowered a thickly muscled arm down through the hole and held out a plain wooden box about ten inches square.

She took it and lifted the lid. A tangle of gems in various settings winked at her from the velvet-lined interior. Her breath stuck at the bottom of her lungs. There were so many of them.

She jumped as Naldo swung down through the hole. Dust clung to his dark jeans and bare chest. He grabbed the box from her hand.

"Hey! Those are my mom's. What are you doing?"

"They're part of the estate."

"But you said your dad gave them to her. That makes them hers."

Naldo tucked the box under his arm. "I told you I'll reimburse you their full value." He lifted an arm and shifted the hatch lid back into position. The ceiling was so low he didn't even have to stretch to do it.

A horrible realization dawned on her. *Naldo only came over here to find the jewels.*

Her rib cage suddenly felt too tight for her heart. He'd seduced her, screwed her, lulled her into a deep, contented sleep…

All so he could sneak up into the attic and steal her mother's property.

"Give that back!" Pain rushed through her.

One of Naldo's black brows lifted slightly. "I said I'll give you money for them."

"How will I know it's a fair amount? I need to get them appraised."

"I'll get them appraised."

"No. I don't trust you."

Naldo's lips parted as if she'd slapped him.

"You know I'm a man of honor."

"Oh, do I? I let you sleep with me, and then I wake up in the morning to find you rooting around *my* house!" Her voice had risen to an ungracious shriek. "I don't trust you as far as I could throw you. Thief!"

Naldo held out the box.

She snatched it and stood there, heart pounding.

Towering and regal despite the dust on his skin, Naldo looked down at her. "I'm no thief. Get them appraised. Tell me their value, and you shall receive it in cash." His black eyes flashed.

"I will." She struggled to hold her chin high. Suddenly, challenging Naldo's honor seemed like a *very* bad idea.

He turned and left without another word, ducking his head to descend the cramped staircase. Her arms tightened around the wooden box and its sharp edges dug into her skin.

Her dream come true had morphed into a nightmare.

"Good grief. Those Victorians did get creative, didn't they?" The jeweler, an older man with a bald head and a large belly, held up yet another ornate monstrosity. "Someone right around 1880 had very inventive taste, I'll say. Where did you say these are from?"

"Family heirlooms," Anna murmured.

"Can't say I recognize any of the work. Your family must have worked with a jeweler who isn't a known name. A few of these pieces are older, though. This one, for example…" He held up a brooch. A yellow gem ringed with blue stones in a heavy, golden setting. Ugly as all the others.

"This one could be eighteenth century, if I'm not mistaken. There's no wear on it, but that's not so unusual with jewelry. It wasn't made to be worn every day. And this ring—" He picked up a simple gold band with a red stone poking out of it. "It could be a good reproduction. In fact, it must be, let's face it, but it's in the style of, well, the Elizabethan era." He raised his eyebrows and chuckled. "Any actors or actresses in your family?"

"Their value. What are they worth?" Anna spoke between gritted teeth. Naldo's family treasures, sprawled on the worn black velvet of the appraiser's desk, looked naked, tragic, shamefully exposed to the mocking eyes of someone never meant to see them.

"Jeez. Hard to say without knowing the provenance. You don't have any paperwork to go along with them?"

"No."

"I'll be frank. There isn't much of a market for this high-

Victorian costume-type stuff, but at least some of the gems are real, so I'll give you a hundred and fifty thousand for the lot."

Anna gasped.

"Cashier's check okay?" He put down his magnifying glass.

Money that didn't come from Naldo. More than enough, too. Her skin prickled with temptation.

But she knew she couldn't take it. And she didn't trust this guy, either.

"How much do I owe you for the appraisal?" She reached into her bag for her checkbook, knowing she probably didn't have enough left in the account.

"It wasn't much of an appraisal since I didn't give you a real value for anything, so it's on the house. And, you know what? I'll give you a hundred and seventy-five because you seem like a sweet girl." He leaned toward her, his patchouli aftershave stealing through the air to stifle her.

Anna leapt to her feet, grasped the jewels in untidy handfuls and heaped them back in the crude wooden box. She should never have brought them here. "They're not mine to sell. They belong to the family. I'll talk to them about it." She sped out of the store before he made any more tempting offers.

Could she sell Naldo's family heirlooms away from the estate while he was willing to pay for them? He certainly deserved it.

"You took them to the jeweler right on Main Street?" Irritation made Naldo's hands curl into fists as he stood in the doorway of the cottage. He'd seen her return and come over right away.

"It was the closest place, and it had a sign saying 'appraisals' in the window." Anna held her trim chin high.

"That dump is practically a pawn shop. I'm surprised he didn't offer you cash for them."

Her head kicked back a little. Her pale hair was pulled into a knot that revealed her lovely slim neck, which right now he was tempted to strangle. Did she want everyone in town to know his father gave the family jewels to his lover?

Why was she so damn quiet? "He did offer cash, didn't he?"

"Yes. A hundred and seventy-five thousand." She licked her pale pink lips.

He snorted. "Pathetic. They're worth five times that. Thank God you weren't fool enough to take it."

Her eyebrows shot up. "Are they really?"

"What?" Naldo was using every ounce of self-control not to charge into the cottage and seize the box, where it lay right on the kitchen table for all to see.

"Worth nearly a million."

He hesitated. "At least. Some of them are as old as… Where did you tell him they came from?"

"Family." She narrowed those penetrating blue eyes and crossed her arms over her perky chest. The action pulled her loose T-shirt tight over nipples he now knew were the exact same color as her lips. "I said they came from family."

"*My* family?" He shoved all thoughts of nipples back where they belonged. His family's honor was on the line here.

"Mine, actually. In case you've forgotten, they belong to *my* mother."

"We both know where they really belong. And you should know better than to take them to a local jeweler who might put two and two together and figure out where they came from."

"Why shouldn't he know the truth?" She cocked her head.

Naldo blinked. Her obstinacy made him so exasperated he could barely think straight. "Because…" He spoke through gritted teeth. "My family's *private* business is just that, *private*. The last thing either of us needs is for the press to get wind of what went on between my father and your mother."

"Why on earth would the press care about what two middle-aged people were doing on their own time?"

"Because my father is Robert De Leon."

Her eyes narrowed to slits. "And my mother was his *cook*. That's it, isn't it? You're ashamed that your father had an affair with a 'servant.' You're just like your snobbish sister. You really do think that my mother was so far beneath him that—"

"You know I have the highest regard for your mother." Naldo cut her off and took a step into the tiny kitchen. "But you know as well as I do that the press will turn it into a tawdry scandal. Do you truly want your mother being remembered as that cook who slept with her boss?"

Anna blinked and stared at him for a moment before replying. "Perhaps it's better than her not being remembered at all."

"Your mother's memory will always be cherished here."

"No, it won't. You're trying to stamp out every trace of her. You want to buy the cottage, you want to buy back the jewels, you want to put everything back exactly the way it was before your father had the temerity to fall in love with someone other than your precious mother. You're so hung up on your own fairy-tale ideal of your father's life that you don't want to deal with the reality."

She took a step toward him, eyes flashing. "Life isn't black and white like your polo uniform, Naldo. You can't take reality and trim it and tweak it into what you want. Real life has shades of gray. It's messy and untidy, and sometimes inconvenient, but it's *real* and you can't just throw money at it and make it go away."

Naldo hesitated. Too right—he was tired of life being a mess. For a decade he'd been torn between loyalty to his proud but difficult mother, and deep love for the caring father who found happiness with the wrong woman. All he wanted to do now was clean the slate and start over.

And Anna saw right through him.

A surge of irritation warred with a sudden disturbing urge to silence this maddening woman with a fast, hard kiss.

But he'd gone down that road before and it certainly hadn't improved matters.

"How much do you want for the jewels and the cottage?"

She settled her hands on her slim hips and stuck out her chest. Something fresh sparked in her eyes. "You mean how much will it take to get me to shut up and leave? How much hush money do I require?" Her breasts heaved under her shirt.

He ignored the thickening sensation in his groin. "You know that's not what I mean. I just want to compensate you fairly."

"So you can make sure you'll never be troubled by me again? So I won't turn up again like a bad penny, looking for more money and reminding you—and everyone else— that the majestic De Leon family has a skeleton in the closet? I've a good mind to go to the papers right now and tell them the whole story."

Naldo froze. "Your mother would never have done that."

"No. She knew her place, didn't she? The faithful family retainer, true to her beloved lord and master. So circumspect that she never even dared to confide in her own daughter."

A flush covered her neck, and he could see her breath coming faster. Was she going to cry? "I think it's disgraceful that your father supposedly loved her for so long and never offered to marry her. Like she wasn't worthy of him. Everyone thinks the great Robert De Leon was such a chivalrous knight of old, faithful to the cherished memory of his beautiful sainted wife. I'd love to let them know exactly what kind of man he really was."

Naldo instinctively took a step forward.

"Don't touch me!" Anna leapt back as if he threatened to bite her. "Get out! Leave me alone."

She *was* going to cry. Naldo stiffened. Part of him wanted to grab her and shake her until she saw reason. Part of him wanted to take her in his arms and console her, and part of him wanted to peel off her clothes and—

"Get out!"

He turned on his heel and left. There was no arguing with a madwoman. Especially when every rational thought you summoned was interrupted by a stray urge to kiss the words right out of her infuriatingly sensual and shockingly insolent mouth.

He swung himself into his car and closed the door with a satisfying slam. His father's mistakes should be a harsh lesson to him. An untidy emotional entanglement had laid him open to the risk of scandal, and ultimately had killed him. Naldo had no doubt his father would still be alive if it wasn't for Letty Marcus.

He'd decided early on that he would never let a woman tie his heart up in one of her nightgown ribbons.

Right now he needed an ice-cold shower to cool his temper and his blood and get everything back exactly where it should be.

Under control.

The next morning, Naldo was eating a grapefruit in the breakfast room when he heard the telltale *click-click* of Isabela's mules on the wood. His spine stiffened.

"Morning, sweet brother."

"Hey." He smoothed out the local paper on the table.

"It's taking an awfully long time to get rid of Ms. Marcus, isn't it? I'd have thought you'd have her bags packed and shipped by now." Isabela slid into the chair opposite him.

"Me, too. I don't know why she's being so difficult." He flipped the page. "But she'll sell. Trust me."

"I'm not entirely sure I do trust you."

Naldo's gaze snapped up in time to see Isabela winking at him as she reached for some toast.

"What do you mean by that?"

"She's pretty."

"So?"

"And you're a man." She snipped off a piece of dry toast with her teeth.

"I have no interest in Anna beyond securing the land for the family." He grabbed his juice glass and took a swig. His eggs lay heavy in his stomach.

"Mmm-hmm." Isabela reached for the butter. "Though you don't seem to be in any hurry, from what I can see. Where exactly did you spend last night?"

"In my bed."

"I mean the night before this one." Her black eyes glittered. "You went out, oh, around three, and came back for breakfast."

"Sweet of you to be concerned about my whereabouts." He sipped his coffee.

"Oh, I'm concerned, all right. The last thing this family needs is more scandal."

"There was no scandal last time. Mother's death was an accident, remember?" His chest tightened.

"You were just a kid. You have no idea what Daddy did to hush everything up. He paid off the police, he *bought* the local paper. Are you willing to do the same?"

"I have no need to do anything."

"Oh, really? How will you feel if the papers report that you're sleeping out in the servants' quarters like dear old Dad?"

"Why would I care? I'm not married. I can sleep where I want."

"With the cook's daughter?"

"Nothing wrong with cooking. We all have to eat. Besides, Anna doesn't work here. She's a successful businesswoman."

Isabela's lips twisted into a little mocking smile. "Oh, dear. Things are rather worse than I suspected. But I know you, Naldo, partly because you're my brother, and partly because you are so exactly like our beloved father. The family name is a brand you'll live and die by, and you'll do anything to prevent it being tarnished, in the papers or anywhere else."

Naldo inhaled slowly. *True.* "What are you driving at?"

"Now that Daddy is gone, all the people he paid off and hushed up over the years are heaving a sigh of relief. What if they get chatty? If word gets out about what happened to Mother?" She leaned forward. "And why it happened? The family name will be legendary for all the wrong reasons. I know you'd hate that."

Isabela rose from her chair, gathering her gauzy dressing gown. She swept behind him.

"What are you doing?"

"You look tense, sweetheart." She dug her thumbs into his shoulders. "Poor Naldo. Even these broad shoulders will be strained by the weighty burden of responsibility you've inherited. I don't envy you. I honestly don't."

Pain and pleasure mingled as she massaged his tight, sore flesh. It felt good. "Where did you learn how to massage?"

"I haven't always lived alone, you know."

"No? So how come you've never married? You're nearly forty."

"Thirty-three," she snapped.

"Yeah, right." He couldn't help smiling. "If you say so. But seriously, you have someone?"

"No. Not now." A note of sadness in her voice surprised him. "I don't think I'd ever dare take a chance on marriage. Not after what happened to Mother. My illusions about love and marriage were shattered at a tender age."

"I didn't know you felt that way." It was true Isabela had taken their mother's death even harder than he had. She hadn't been home for more than a few days since it happened. Isabela was a carbon copy of their mother. She'd gained weight in the last few years, and was now a lusher, fuller version of her. Their mother had fiercely supported her dream of being a singer, in the face of their father's opposition, perhaps as a way of chasing her own thwarted dream of performing on the world's great stages.

But Isabela's singing career had gone nowhere. She'd directed one or two small operas. She wasn't married. She must be lonely. His heart contracted with pity for her. "What do you want to do with your life, Izzy?"

"As I said before, I just want a quiet little place of my own. A few hundred acres to build a barrier between myself and the cruel world."

He snorted. "A few hundred acres in Europe? Maybe we should just invade Monaco and take it over?"

"I know, I know. But if you sold this place and moved the family back there… You'd love it, Naldo. People know how to live in the old style. They understand the importance of tradition—"

"I love it *here*."

"Oh, Naldo. You're so stubborn. Just like Daddy."

"And Mom. And you."

Isabela laughed. "I guess we're all kind of hard to live with. It does feel like the end of an era, though, doesn't it?"

"Or the beginning of a new one. I know what I'm doing. I've managed the estate for seven years."

"I don't doubt it." She lifted her hands off his shoulders. Oddly, they were more tense than when she'd started.

"Mother's jewels." Her clipped words made his neck tighten. "I looked in her dresser, and they're not there. They've always been there."

"She died ten years ago."

"I know, but Daddy never moved them before. Are they in the bank?"

"Why, are you thinking they'd look good on you?"

"Well, perhaps a piece or two. To remember Mother by."

He cocked his head. "What if I want them for my wife?"

Right now he didn't even want a wife. But one day he would marry and his wife should enjoy the legacy of a De Leon bride.

Isabela pressed a hand to her heart and inhaled deeply, eyes closed. "You know, Naldo, it hurts me right *here*, that everything our parents owned belongs to you, and nothing belongs to me. Do you think it's fair?"

"No, I don't think it's fair. But I can see how it's practical. If you divide everything up with each generation, sooner or later there's nothing left."

Isabela lifted her proud head and looked out the window, then snapped her gaze back to his. Her eyes glittered with sudden tears. "Don't be selfish. You know I look just like Mother. I'd so love to have a piece or two, to remember how things were...before..."

Save it for La Scala.

"Good luck. Dad gave them all to Letty Marcus." He said it coldly. If Isabela wanted opera-style drama, she could have it in spades.

"What?" Her tears vanished.

"He gave her the lot. I'm not sure if it was piece by piece, or all at once, but Anna has them now. I'm trying to buy them back."

"Dieu." She stared at him. "He must have lost his mind completely. Surely it's not legal? They weren't mentioned in the will. Why can't you just *take* them back?"

Tried that. He drummed his fingertips on the table. "I don't think that's the honorable thing to do."

"Honor be damned! We're talking about the family heritage here."

"Trust me. I know. I offered her cash, but she's as stubborn as a De Leon."

"She won't sell?"

"She'll sell. I'll make sure of it."

Already afternoon and the packing was not going well. Anna scraped her damp hair off her hot neck and wrapped it into a knot. She had no use for the old-fashioned bedside clock with its painted enamel design, since she had a programmable digital one, but could she just throw it away?

No way.

Yard sale?

Hardly a prime location.

So the clock still sat on the simple wood nightstand. The Lladro porcelain figures and hand-knitted doilies similarly balked at leaving the mantel in the sitting room. The scented collection of shell-shaped soaps in large beach shells refused to give up their multiyear residence on the shelf above the bathroom sink.

Her mother's possessions had ganged up and decided to stay.

"Anna!"

Naldo's deep voice, right under the open window of her mother's bedroom, made her jump. *What now?*

It was bad enough that she couldn't seem to get that forceful voice out of her head, now she had to deal with the face and body that went with it?

She leaned out the window. "You rang?"

"Hey." A smile sneaked across his wide, sensual mouth.

How could he have the audacity to look pleased to see her? He must be up to something.

"Hey yourself."

"Can I come in?"

"Can I prevent you?"

With a smile he disappeared from view, walking around to the front of the house.

She scanned the front of her T-shirt and shorts. Stain-free.

His heavy footsteps on the stairs were echoed in the heavy beat of her heart. She was *not* going to get swept off her feet by him this time.

He materialized in the doorway, all windblown black hair, flashing dark eyes and tanned muscles barely contained by a black polo shirt.

Great. She sucked in a breath. "How may I help you?"

"Just thought I'd see how the packing is going." He scanned the room. A line appeared between his brows.

"As you can see, it's not going so well."

"Need a hand?"

His expression of good cheer didn't fool her for an instant. "No thanks."

He licked his lips. She ignored a tiny flare of heat in her belly. "I've been thinking."

Uh-oh.

He picked up a china cat off the nightstand and turned it over, as if to read the maker's mark on the bottom.

Probably said Wal-Mart.

"I should take the jewels to Breathley Brothers in St. George. They deal in fine historic gems, and they can do an up-to-date appraisal that incorporates provenance. I do have paperwork for many of the pieces, after all."

"And there I was, thinking you came here to help me clean." She put her hands on her hips. "I was just about to ask you to help me scrub the bathroom floor."

His dimples appeared. "Celia would do a better job of that. I can send her over, if you like. I'm not sure I'd even fit in that bathroom."

An image of Naldo's big, bronzed body squeezed into the tiny shower stall assaulted her imagination.

He took a step forward and his rich male scent crept up on her. "I want our arrangement to be completely fair."

Fair? Nothing about this was fair. For a start it wasn't fair that Naldo always had such a discombobulating effect on her.

The image in her mind shifted into deeper focus. Thick droplets of warm water cascading over the hair-roughened skin of his powerful thighs.

She inhaled sharply. "Maybe I could take them."

His brows lowered. "Perhaps we could go together."

"When?"

"Right now." He crossed his arms, in a gesture matching hers. His thick forearms tugged at the front of his black shirt, pulling it tighter over his well-developed pecs.

She crossed her arms higher to cover the tightening of her naughty nipples.

"I guess I'd better get changed."

"I don't know why. I think you look lovely like that."

"I'm not sure your snooty jeweler will agree. They probably frown on cutoffs."

"Let them frown all they want; they won't turn away my business." His lips lifted into a half smile.

So true. An old name and even older money guaranteed you the best of everything. Naldo had probably never heard the word *no* in his life.

"I'll change anyway."

"I'll watch." His eyes narrowed as his smile broadened.

"You will not!" Her protest accompanied a curl of heat in her belly. The thought of those dangerous dark eyes on her, appraising, admiring…

"Wait downstairs."

Naldo pouted slightly before turning for the stairs. He ducked, stooping his broad shoulders as he went down the tiny staircase.

Her nipples stung as she slid her T-shirt over them, and her panties were already damp. Just being in the room with Naldo made her pant like a preteen at a rock concert.

How was she supposed to stand the half-hour drive to St. George cooped up in his tiny car with him?

She needed a chastity belt.

And the next best thing was a dress from her mother's closet. Surely she wouldn't think lusty thoughts if she was wearing clothes that belonged to her *mom*. She flipped past a pretty floral dress and a low-backed white one, then lifted a splashy polka-dot number from its hanger.

Perfect. It was the kind of thing that only her mom could pull off. Naldo would certainly be too weirded out to give her any smoldering looks in this.

Six

Naldo frowned as Anna emerged through the front door, jewel box in hand, to where he paced on the lawn. "You're wearing *that*?"

"You don't like it?" She did a twirl, which caused the polka-dotted skirt to flare out around her.

"It's okay, it's just that you look like…"

Your mother.

The unspoken words crackled in the air.

Her mother had loved patterns, bright colors, girly details. A stark contrast to Anna's own preference for pastels and simple sheath dresses. The fitted forties-style dress was a size too big, but with the belt cinched in it looked… festive.

The look of distress on Naldo's face gave her a warm glow of satisfaction.

"Do that again," he said, with an unreadable expression.

"What?"

"Twirl."

She twirled, hoping to see consternation furrow his majestic brow again.

She was annoyed to confront a smug look of satisfaction.

"Suits you." He strode to his Alfa Romeo and tugged open the passenger-side door. "You should show off your shape more often."

Anna bristled with irritation as she lowered herself into the seat and strapped herself in, nipples thrumming inside the fitted bodice of her mother's dress.

After he returned from his house with the papers, Naldo's eyes fell to the wooden box cradled in her lap. "Why don't you put one of the pieces on? That dress could use some earrings."

"No thanks. I don't want to get attached." She shot him a loaded glance.

His lips quirked into a smile. "Understandable."

During the drive they chatted, mostly about the estate and Naldo's plans to improve and upgrade using the latest technology and scientific research. Anna answered his questions about her work with genuine enthusiasm—she'd been damn good at it, after all—and managed to deflect his curiosity about her future plans with blurry answers and more questions for him.

It was cute how he could talk about his beloved estate and its people and places for hours. His love for them was obviously deep, ingrained and heartfelt. What would it be like to have a man care about you with that kind of intensity?

She tore her eyes from his proud profile. She knew better than to entertain any thoughts about Naldo loving her. That was the road to heartbreak.

Naldo parked in front of an elegant Queen Anne house in a leafy part of St. George. The jeweler was so low-profile that they didn't even use a sign. Naldo had called ahead on his cell, and they were greeted at the door by a young man in a white linen suit, who was on a first-name basis with Naldo.

Was this a setup? Had Naldo roped some friend of his into pretending to be a jeweler? Was he going to provide a false, low valuation so he could buy the gems back on the cheap?

Suspicious thoughts crept around her mind as she climbed the wide, deep steps of the house, her polka-dot skirt draping around her knees.

The man in the white suit ushered them into a cool, shady drawing room filled with Victorian antiques and offered them iced tea. Naldo refused, but Anna accepted a glass, then wished she hadn't when more wary thoughts sneaked over her.

Is it poisoned? Drugged? Is this part of Naldo's cunning plot to be rid of me once and for all?

The increasingly lunatic direction of her thoughts, and the fact that she was wearing what amounted to a fancy-dress costume, suddenly struck her as hilarious. She was struggling not to laugh out loud when a tall, slim, elderly man in a brown pinstripe suit walked into the room, leaning lightly on a cane.

"Mr. De Leon." He shook Naldo's hand. "Good to see you again."

"This is Anna Marcus." Naldo indicated Anna, who stepped forward to shake his hand.

"The future Mrs. De Leon?" The elderly man smiled.

"No." Both Anna and Naldo spat the reply at once. Anna felt a flicker of irritation that he was so quick to dismiss the possibility. Then she was mad at herself for wishing he hadn't.

"Oh. I beg your pardon. How may I help you?"

Naldo glanced at Anna's lap, where she still held the box in a vise grip. "We're seeking valuation for some family jewels. We would like to know the correct market price."

"I see. Bring the gems to my desk, please." He walked stiffly to a large, leather-topped table with several vintage-looking pieces of equipment on it.

Anna crossed the room, clutching the box. She laid it on the leather surface. She hovered, apprehensive, as he raised the lid.

A frown crossed his weathered face. "I've seen these pieces before." He looked up at Anna, who felt her eyebrows shoot up. She heard Naldo shift in his chair, behind her. "The late Mr. De Leon brought them to me seeking appraisal some years ago."

"For insurance?" Naldo frowned. "He never believed in it."

"I don't know the reason, but I gave him a detailed appraisal at that time. Let me get my notes."

The man who'd opened the door brought a thick file, and the appraiser proceeded to read from a detailed report he'd prepared a few years earlier.

Anna's jaw was in her lap by the time he'd finished going over the pieces one by one—lamenting the careless storage and admonishing Naldo, who he assumed to be the owner, for tossing them in a crude box. Three of the pieces were over three hundred years old. One necklace contained a famous diamond known as the Star of the Sea, once owned by an Indian maharaja and brought to the States by one of Naldo's merchant ancestors. The Victorian pieces the other jeweler had scoffed at were the work of an idiosyncratic but respected American designer whose work now fetched a premium at auction.

When all was said and done, the combined value of the twelve pieces in the box was "priceless." A "fair market value" was determined to be somewhere between two and three million dollars, with unlimited upside potential at auction, depending on the bidders.

"Why weren't they mentioned in the will?" breathed Anna, as she stumbled down the front steps. Naldo was carrying the box. She didn't feel worthy to even touch it any more. He was right, they were *his* family treasures.

"Perhaps he didn't intend for her to keep them." Naldo's expression was stony as he opened her car door.

She buckled in, unease trickling through her, as she waited for him to walk around to his side and climb in.

"So if he just gave them to her, and there's no paper trail…" She tried to make sense of it.

"The gift wouldn't be legal. Taxes must be paid on a gift of this size."

"Oh." Her mother hadn't paid any taxes on a gift like this. She'd done her mom's tax returns for the last ten years.

The gems weren't hers. She wondered if she should feel upset, but she didn't. She'd never had any real right to them.

Naldo had placed the box in the trunk of the car.

He'd repossessed it. And she didn't have the energy to protest.

"I'll have to do some digging around. Find out who they really belong to."

She relaxed a little as he started the engine. As he reversed out of the parking space, he shot a hot, dark glance in her direction.

After they'd driven a couple of blocks, he looked at her again and his eyes skimmed lower, to the plunging neckline of her bold dress, to the cinched-in hourglass of her waist.

Taking possession. He did that well. Already her body responded with a shivery flush of warmth that spread over her skin and deep inside her.

Damn him.

She fixed her eyes on the windshield, only to gasp when he swung the car to the side of the road, threw it into Park and captured her lips in a warm, wet kiss.

Her mind fought back for a split second, but her body capitulated instantly as the stirring male scent of his warm skin crept over her, and his penetrating and forceful kiss plundered her mouth and stole her senses.

She writhed against the pleasurable pressure of the harness seat belt, her nipples humming with arousal. She wriggled in her seat, arching and straining as his big, broad hands roved over the front of her dress, cupping her breasts and stroking her belly.

He lifted the skirt of her dress with one swift movement of his hand, baring her thighs. With her legs splayed against the seat, parted by his hand, she felt wanton, desirable and ready for anything.

Naldo unfastened her seat belt and helped her ease her arms out of it. He hiked her dress up over her waist and dove into her panties, tugging them down as his eager tongue reached for her swollen sex.

As his broad back filled the distance from his seat to hers, she lifted her hips and gave herself to him, mentally begging him to lick and suck her all the way to heaven.

Then she remembered the jewels.

And how Naldo had used sex to get what he wanted.

"Stop!"

If he heard, he showed no sign of it. His tongue slaked her inner thigh, hot and wet, as his fingers roved between the buttons on the front of her dress to press her eager nipples.

She wriggled under the pressure of his lips and fingers, wanting to give herself over to the sensual pleasure of his touch.

He's doing this to distract you. To use you somehow.

"Naldo!"

"What?" His throaty moan was half buried in her thighs.

"Stop this right now! I know what you're up to."

"Driving you…" He broke off, losing his mouth in her chest.

"You're not driving." Her words came out kind of squeaky and breathless as he nipped at her nipples though the polka-dot fabric.

"Wild with desire," he murmured, trailing his face over her breasts.

Well, yes, that and— "Getting my mind off the jewels."

"Sounds like a plan." He nibbled at her neck, sending delicious shivers of arousal over her skin.

"Stop, I mean it."

Something in her voice caught his attention because he did stop. He looked up at her, his big dark eyes shining with desire. He levered himself off her and pulled back, brows lowering.

"I want to get out."

"We're in St. George."

"I know the town. I had a job here during the summer in high school. I'll get a cab back."

"Don't be ridiculous. I'll drive you."

"Drive me home, or drive me wild with desire?"

A wicked gleam shone in his dark eyes. "Both, if you like."

"I'd rather take a cab. You can take the jewels, they're probably yours anyway, but I don't want any more of your kisses."

"Why not?"

His simple question made her pause.

Because you're stealing my heart.

"Because there's no future between us and I don't need to be used right now. I just got divorced and I'm feeling fragile and—"

And you're Naldo De Leon, the one man I've always wanted, but knew I could never have.

"Relax. I'm not trying to cheat you. I'll make sure you're fairly compensated."

There he was again, offering her *money.*

Nothing but money.

He had no intention of giving her anything of himself. Ever.

"If you have fifty dollars," she said shakily, "I'd like to take a cab."

He looked at her for a moment like she'd lost her mind, then leaned his head back on the head rest, his hard jaw jutting out. The thick bulge in his pants caught her attention before she yanked her gaze away.

He reached into his back pocket and tugged out his money clip. He peeled off four fifty-dollar bills.

"I'll never take you anywhere you don't want to go."

"Just one will do." Her face was hot with the humiliation of having to ask him for cash. She lifted one bill from his hand, and he let go of all four so the other three fluttered to his knees. One fell on the floor.

Anna pulled on the door handle and maneuvered her

way out of the car, tugging down her skirt. The bright afternoon sunlight stung her dilated pupils. "Thanks," she rasped, clutching the crisp banknote. "I'll pay you back."

Naldo emitted a low growl, which was silenced by her car door as it closed with an expensive-sounding click.

She set off down the sidewalk, feeling Naldo's eyes on her as she flounced away in her polka dots, his fifty-dollar bill crumpled into her hand.

Maybe her mother couldn't resist the De Leon charm and had settled for being a kind of secret mistress, but she sure wouldn't make the same mistake.

The morning shadows shrank as the sun rose high on yet another day in the cottage. Anna had stopped packing completely. The stuff didn't want to be packed. She didn't have anywhere pressing to go. What was the rush? She'd taken a couple of pieces of her mom's modest china collection to the jeweler/pawn shop owner in town and raised enough to live on for a few days.

And to pay back Naldo his fifty dollars, which she'd stuck in an envelope and placed in the mansion's mailbox.

She lay stretched out on the sofa, flipping through a handwritten recipe book she'd found in one of the kitchen drawers. Was this the one mentioned in the will? Why would there be a special provision that her mom should keep her own recipe book?

It was beautiful, though. Bound in red leather, a special book made to be treasured. No scrawled notes or taped-in newspaper clippings here. Her mom had written the recipes in a careful copperplate hand on the creamy vellum. Pen-and-ink drawings accented with bright watercolors illustrated some of the recipes.

The drawings surprised her. She hadn't known her mom

had artistic talent. But apparently there were a lot of things she hadn't known about her. She bit the inside of her mouth as another wave of raw emotion threatened.

A load roar outside yanked her attention from the smooth pages of the cookbook.

What was that noise?

Anna peered out the window of the cottage.

A lawnmower. Typical. Naldo must have told the gardener to keep on maintaining the property around the cottage as if it was still *his*. Annoyance spurred her to her feet as the mower came into view through the window.

Now that the cottage and the land were all she had, she felt proprietary about them. She'd even started to have stray thoughts about keeping them. She didn't have anywhere else to go right now.

She hurried outside and waved her hands to get the driver to stop. It was a young guy she didn't recognize. "Please don't mow this lawn," she called, striding toward him.

The man frowned. "The grass is getting long."

"Mr. De Leon no longer owns this cottage or the land around it." A flash of fear stung her as she made the bold pronouncement. It didn't feel true.

The young man's eyebrows raised in surprise. "You kidding?"

"Nope. It's mine. My mother used to live here and Robert De Leon left it to her when she died."

"Letty was your mother?"

"Yes."

"Oh." He nodded. "She was very nice." He gave her a strange look, and there was an awkward silence thick with the unspoken words *and you, maybe, aren't so nice.*

Why did it mean so much to her not to have Naldo's employee mow *her* grass?

"Anyway, I'd appreciate it if you didn't mow here for now. I want to grow the grass longer, for a more natural look." She licked her lips awkwardly.

The gardener's brow lowered and a smile tugged at his lips. "More natural?"

"Yes, you know. A Xeriscape."

He looked like he was trying not to laugh. "You're the boss. You don't want it mowed, I won't mow."

Anna gulped. She didn't feel like the boss of anything.

"I'm Ricky, by the way." He looked at her steadily.

"Oh, hi, I'm Anna." She walked closer and held out her hand, mortified that she'd forgotten even common politeness in her grim quest to defend her little stronghold.

"Hi, Anna." Something twinkled in his eyes as he gave her hand a firm shake. Amusement. Anticipation of the fireworks display he'd see when he told Naldo?

She gulped.

A big white Mercedes sedan pulled into view, and she gulped again when she saw Isabela's face in the open driver's side window.

"Gotta go," said Ricky. He sped away on the mower before Isabela adjusted her dark glasses and stepped out.

In a floaty chiffon jacket and wide-legged pants, she looked comically overdressed as she picked her way across the overgrown grass in her high-heeled shoes.

"Anna." She smiled. "I must apologize for the other night." She lifted her huge sunglasses to reveal big brown eyes. "I was feeling rather emotional. It's been a hard time, Daddy's death, you know. Coming home for the first time in ages." She waved a ring-laden hand in the air. "I suspect I was rather rude."

You could say that. Anna wondered if this visit was really about making amends.

Isabela gave an apologetic smile. "I'm an artist. I can be a little temperamental. Truce?" She held out her hand.

Anna decided to give her the benefit of the doubt. After all, Isabela's bluntness had clued her in to the truth.

She shook Isabela's soft hand. "It's a tough time. I'll miss your dad. He was a pretty amazing guy. And I actually appreciate you filling me in on the situation between him and my mom. I really had no idea. A lot of things make sense now."

Isabela nodded. "And you have this cottage." She gestured at it. "You own more of the estate than I do." An odd laugh peeled out of her. "Funny, isn't it?"

Anna felt a stab of pity. The look in Isabela's face showed that it hurt more than her glib words let on. "It is odd that you don't inherit. Especially since you're the oldest."

"I'm a mere girl. Patriarchal to the core, that's the De Leon family. That's why it's such a shocker that Daddy left land to your mother. She must have held quite a sway over him."

"Or maybe he just felt guilty that he didn't marry her."

"Yes." Isabela looked thoughtful. "But he gave her the jewels, at any rate, and that's why I'm here. I'd like to buy a piece or two, purely for sentimental reasons."

Anna frowned. Did Isabela not know that Naldo had them now? That they supposedly belonged to him?

"Naldo has them."

"Oh, I know. But they're yours. Daddy paid a gift tax on them five years ago." She tilted her elegantly coiffed head.

Really? Interesting that Naldo hadn't shared that tidbit of information with her. "So they're legally mine?"

"Absolutely. And of course my darling brother intends to buy them from you to restore them to the estate, but I'd so like the pretty ring with the lion on it. And that old yellow diamond in the funny setting."

"I guess I don't feel they're mine to sell, even though they might be legally. Perhaps after I sell them back to Naldo, you can buy them from him?"

Isabela pouted slightly, dimpling her chin. "My brother can be terribly difficult. He probably won't want them to leave the sacred turf of the estate. I did inherit some spending money when Daddy died, so I can pay what they're worth. They are my family treasures, too, you know."

Anna did feel bad for her. How would she handle being shunted aside so a brother could inherit everything? But she knew how strongly Naldo felt about the jewels. Naldo felt strongly about everything. "Seriously, I don't even have them. You'd better talk to Naldo."

Isabela chewed the plastic end of her sunglasses between straight white teeth. "Could we go inside for a moment?"

"Um, sure." Anna led the way through the kitchen and into the tiny sitting room. Isabela looked at the old sofa as if it might bite, then lowered herself onto it.

"This cottage is a sweet little place, isn't it?" She glanced around, a slight grimace shadowing her haughty features. Anna saw the faded paint, inexpensive knick-knacks and mismatched colors through Isabela's critical eyes. Somehow it made her love them more.

"Yes, it is."

"But I know you don't want to stay. You have a business to run, a life to lead." She raised large, slightly watery eyes to Anna. "I had those things once, but my career…" She broke off and fanned her face with a hand, looking dangerously close to tears. "It's a tough business and I'm not getting any younger. As you heard me say to Naldo, all I want now is a place to call home."

She closed her eyes and inhaled deeply. "This could be my home."

Anna blinked rapidly. "What?"

Isabela fixed her with a doe-eyed gaze. "Will you sell the cottage and the land to me? It would be an act of sisterhood."

Anna's brain was starting to feel overloaded. Sisterhood? With Isabela De Leon? What on earth was she up to? Trying to snatch the land away from Naldo so she had a claim to the property?

"I can't. Naldo offered to buy it first and I know it means a lot to him."

Isabela's lip quivered. "I feel so…rootless and alone. With nowhere to call home."

Trust me, I know the feeling.

"I'm not even sure if I'm going to sell. I'm having a hard time packing because I'm so attached to the place."

"You might keep it?" Isabela's face snapped back into sharp focus. "You mean, actually live here?"

"Yes." As she said it, the casual thought took on the weight of a serious possibility.

The only real snag would be proximity to Naldo.

"You can't keep it." Isabela's loud voice rang off the walls. "My brother wouldn't hear of it. Naldo will fight in court to preserve the integrity of the estate. There's no way he'll accept the existence of a one-acre *hole* in his beloved kingdom. You might think you're going to keep it, but sooner or later, he'll get his way and you'll end up with *nothing*."

The final word was growled through closed teeth.

Anna shivered.

Isabela laughed. "I'll tell you a secret. Naldo sent me here. He thinks I'm here trying to persuade you to sell to him. I even told him I'd ask you to sell it to me, and he loved the idea, thought it was hilarious."

She leaned forward. "Men don't take us seriously." Her eyes narrowed. "They think we're just pretty playthings here to serve their needs. When they're done with us, they toss us aside. I need to protect myself, and you should protect yourself." She tilted her head. "I know he slept in your bed."

Anna gritted her teeth. Had Naldo told her?

"Don't flatter yourself that he cares about you. Naldo means to have this property one way or another, and he *will* have it. Protect yourself."

She rose to her feet with a fluttering of chiffon and shoved her black glasses back on. Her heels tapped on the linoleum as she stalked out of the house, leaving Anna still perched in a living room chair.

Isabela left a trail of unease—and cloying scent—in her wake.

Had Naldo *sent* his sister to persuade her with stories of "sentimental reasons" and sexist exclusion? She didn't believe for a moment that Isabela wanted the cottage for herself. She might not have the limitless means of her brother, but Isabela could undoubtedly buy a ten-thousand-square-foot beachside mansion without even straining her bank accounts.

She was up to something, and it seemed very likely that Naldo was behind it. He'd already proved he was devious enough to use kisses, even sex, to get his way. What next?

She was going to let him know exactly what she thought of his little plan.

She stomped inside and picked up the phone. The pink, heart-shaped piece of paper with Naldo's number still lay on the counter and she punched it in.

"Hi, Pilar, it's Anna, where can I find Naldo?" she asked as politely as she could.

"He left for the south orchards, out by the water tower, about three hours ago. They're putting in some new rows there."

"Thanks."

She grabbed her keys.

Seven

Anna spotted the golf cart Naldo's father always used to get around the estate—painted burgundy with RDL emblazoned in cream letters—just off the dirt road at the end of a row of newly transplanted trees. He must be out barking orders at the poor peons in his employ.

She tried not to let the sweet rich orange scent dissipate her mood of raw indignation as she strode through the grove. At last she came upon a knot of men digging evenly spaced holes to accept a truckload of new transplants.

She squinted in the bright sun, trying to spot that unmistakably imperious profile amongst the suntanned workers. Then she saw him.

Naldo knelt in the sandy soil, an expression of rapt concentration on his hard features. His broad hands patted the dirt into place around a fragile young transplant. As she watched the tender care with which he treated the plant and the freshly turned earth that held it, her breath caught in her lungs.

The trees are family to us.

She steeled herself against a wave of sappy emotion that would not help her in any way. "Naldo."

"Anna." He sat back on his heels. A perplexed frown crossed his forehead, then his eyes narrowed. "You've come to apologize."

"Apologize?" Her blood pressure shot up. "Are you kidding me?"

He looked past her, to where she could still hear the sound of shovels moving the soft soil. "Let's walk." He rose to his feet, dusting off his pants.

Dressed all in black, shirtsleeves rolled over his broad forearms to accommodate the afternoon heat, Naldo looked effortlessly elegant. She wore a pretty white sundress she'd found in her mother's closet. She couldn't help thinking they must make rather a dashing couple, strolling down the lush rows of perfectly maintained orange trees.

An illusion. Black and white, opposites in every way, she and Naldo had nothing in common other than a vested interest in one dusty acre of land.

"No one will come down these rows," he said, once the thunking of shovels was no longer audible. He turned to face her.

"You know why I'm here," she said. "I think it's pathetic that you sent your sister to talk me into selling out. I wouldn't have thought that was your style, Naldo, sending a woman to fight your battles. I guess you've changed."

A line appeared between Naldo's dark brows. "What on earth are you talking about?"

"Isabela. She paid a visit to the cottage. I especially enjoyed the part where she appealed to me out of sisterhood."

Naldo looked at her like she was crazy. His eyes narrowed to black slits. "Sisterhood?"

"She warned me about you. She told me you'd stop at nothing to get the land, and I'd better watch out."

Naldo laughed, long and hard. "She knows me, all right. Are you scared?" His face creased into a grin that brought out his dimples.

"I'm not scared of anyone or anything." She held her head high.

"I believe you. It's one of the many things I like about you." His infuriating grin persisted.

Anger bubbled in her chest. "And, Isabela happened to mention that your father did give my mother the jewels legally."

Naldo's smile vanished. "Yes. He paid the gift tax. They were hers, and now they're yours. I apologize for not telling you myself but I only learned the news this morning and I've been out in the groves ever since."

"So." She cleared her throat. "I have a proposal. I'd like to sell you the jewels, and keep the land and cottage." The idea had occurred to her almost at the moment she said it. It didn't mean she *had* to stay in the cottage, but it would be there for her, a home to come back to, and she'd still have money to get her life back on track.

She held her breath.

"No."

"Why not?"

"All or nothing. I must have that land back."

"That was a nice touch having Isabela pretend she wanted it for herself."

Naldo's forehead furrowed slightly. "I had nothing to do with Isabela coming to visit you. If she tried to buy it from you it was for her own reasons."

"She said she wanted to live there."

"Did she now?" His mouth hitched into a wry smile. "Since that is about as likely as me wanting to live there, she has some other plan. As you know, she'd love me to sell the whole estate. No doubt she planned to sell it to developers or something to force my hand."

"She couldn't do that. There's no road easement."

"I know." His satisfied smile irked her. "But I'm disturbed that you checked. It seems that all the women around here are trying to sell off a piece of my private paradise. You can't trust anyone." He lifted a brow.

"I already know I can't trust you. You'll stop at nothing to get what you want."

"Spoken like someone who knows me well." His eyes sparkled with amusement. "And since we're on the subject, how about three million five hundred thousand dollars for the land, the cottage, the jewels and the cookbook."

Anna's lips parted and a tingle of astonishment sneaked up her neck.

"I can have the money for you today. In cash, or wired into the account of your choice." His expression had turned more serious. "I'm sure we both want to get this resolved."

"Yes." Her word emerged as a breathy whisper.

Three and a half million dollars.

They'd walked out of the grove of newly planted trees into an early-season grove now in full white-petaled bloom.

The thought of all that money in her overdrawn bank account...freaked her out. Suddenly shaky, she inhaled a deep lungful of the rich sweet fragrance. The bright blossoms shone like stars among the dark, shiny leaves.

"These trees will set a lot of fruit this year," she murmured.

"They will." His forehead furrowed and he looked at her curiously.

Three and a half million dollars. It was more than enough to do anything. Or nothing. She'd be independent, free of obligation to anyone. She could walk out of here and never look back.

The thought punched her in the gut like a blow. If she took the money she'd never see this place again.

She hesitated as the blossom-scented air filled her senses. All around her, miles of trees in various stages of blooming and fruiting dug their roots down into the rich soil, drawing life, giving nourishment and strength.

"You would give me the money and I would just…go." Without planning to, she spoke the painful thought aloud. The anguish she heard in her voice made her heart seize tighter.

"Yes." Something odd flickered in Naldo's eyes.

Naldo wanted to sever her roots. To cut her adrift in the harsh world that had bruised her like a tender fruit in the wrong hands.

She couldn't breathe right. Maybe it was the orange oil in the air, or the bright sun in her eyes, but she couldn't seem to get enough oxygen to her brain to say the word *yes*.

Naldo stood like a statue, regal and imposing, his black shirt open at the neck to reveal his bronze throat. She watched his Adam's apple move as he spoke. "Four million."

His voice emerged low. Not a question, not even a demand. There was something odd in his tone that further hindered her ability to form a coherent thought. There was something even stranger in his eyes as he took a step forward and seized her hand.

The warm, firm touch of his long fingers made her catch her breath. She dug her feet into the sandy soil, trying to get a grip on something, anything. His hand closed around hers and he took another step that brought his chest within inches of hers.

She struggled to find words but the beating of her heart was too loud and the blood rushed to her brain. Naldo took hold of her chin between thumb and forefinger and tilted her face to his. His brow furrowed and his eyes narrowed as he studied her face. She moved her lips, hoping that some sensible words would find their way to them, but no sound came out.

Naldo's gaze dropped to her mouth, his eyelids lowered a fraction and he inhaled…then took her mouth in a deep, penetrating kiss that made her belly quiver.

Her fingers clawed into his thick hair as he tipped her head back. His mouth devoured hers hungrily, his face pushed against hers, skin on skin, the rich, musky scent of him mingling with the fragrant blossoms to overpower her senses.

As he deepened the soul-stealing kiss, she ran her fingers over the roping muscles of his back and tugged at his shirt, sneaking her fingertips down his spine and into his waistband.

Instantly she felt him thicken and harden against her. He let out a low groan and a broad hand roved down her dress to cup her breast, then lower to test the curve of her rear. He squeezed her against him and she gasped. So big and powerful, yet so gentle and tender, Naldo took her breath away.

She tore at the front of his shirt, pulling the buttons roughly from their holes, scratching at the firm, tan skin beneath. Naldo unzipped her dress in one swift motion, and they both shoved it and her panties down over her waist and legs, urgency building in the orange-scented air.

She fumbled with the front of Naldo's pants, and he unzipped them and shucked them, letting them fall as he gathered her in his arms. Naked.

A fierce, wild shiver ran right through her like a breeze in the windless air.

Naldo lowered her gently to the soft sandy ground carpeted with scented orange blossom petals. He lay down beside her, his eyes dark slits of desire, as he ran his fingertips over the curve of her waist and along the length of her thigh, triggering painful arousal—until he stopped.

"I don't have a condom." Agony creased his brow.

"I'm on the pill," she murmured, barely able to talk as her body throbbed with longing. "Don't stop."

His middle finger pushed between her thighs and into her moist heat. She moaned as he touched her, her hips lifting to meet his hand. Her nipples ached and her skin hummed with a craving to be to be skin to skin with Naldo De Leon.

With Naldo De Leon.

What was she doing?

He'd offered her four million dollars, and instead of taking the money and running like any sensible person would do, she'd jumped on him and torn off his clothes.

Surely she should—?

His finger tripped a hotwire inside her. She bucked against his hand and let out a strange, animal sound. Naldo silenced her with a hard kiss, his big body moving over hers, muscle heavy on her as his tongue tangled with hers.

She lifted her hips as he entered her, taking him deep. A shudder of profound relief rippled through her. Naldo cupped her head with one hand and kissed her greedily as he plunged deep inside her, driving her further and further into a paradise of sensation.

She writhed against him, moaning and murmuring his name as she climbed higher toward the peak of the most intense emotion she'd ever felt.

I love this man.

Again the thought stole into her mind and this time she didn't shove it away.

Powerful, passionate, fiercely loyal to his proud family and the estate he loved, Naldo was a man like no other.

He dove into her one last time and her climax took her. Like a roller coaster plunging from the highest point, she sped down, screaming, into an abyss of shocking pleasure. Naldo held her tight, his groans echoing in her ears, as she crashed back to earth on the petal-strewn sand.

It was some time—she had no idea how long—before she managed to open her eyes. She met Naldo's black gaze.

I love you.

She crushed the thought back into her brain. No sense making a fool of herself. At least not more than she already had.

She became uncomfortably aware of the gritty ground under her hot, sweaty skin.

Um, what just happened?

Naldo's dimple appeared. "You have a strange effect on me."

"Yeah." She frowned. "I've noticed that."

"And apparently the feeling is mutual." His wide, sensual mouth tilted into a half smile.

"I wouldn't say that…." She feigned a serious expression until Naldo tickled her belly and she broke into a giggle.

"Did I scream?" The thought of the workers one grove over made her clap a hand over her mouth.

"Yes. Most definitely." Humor twinkled in his eyes.

"What if someone heard?" Her eyes widened.

"The trees provide excellent sound insulation. Do you hear anyone rushing to your aid?" He raised a brow.

"No."

"So, as you can see, you're at my mercy." His smile broadened.

"Even if they could hear, I bet your faithful employees would just whistle and pretend they heard nothing." She narrowed her eyes. Her mouth fought a grin.

"It's nice being the boss." He winked. "But then you'd know that."

Anna swallowed. *He still had no idea she was penniless, bankrupt...a failure.*

"Though I don't know how you run a business if you don't like money."

"I like money just fine."

"You could have fooled me." He tilted his head, smiling at her. "I keep trying to give you some, but I can't get you to take it. I guess you have too much already."

If only.

"It's not that I don't want the money..." Her voice trailed off.

"But you're too proud to take it?"

She hesitated. Was it pride? Maybe a little. But it was something else, too. Mushy sentimentality for a place she'd once called home.

An indulgence she couldn't afford.

"I just need to be sure I'm being fairly compensated." She grasped at the first straw that came to mind. "I'm a businesswoman, as you said."

"If you run your business anything like the way you..." he regarded her steadily with those penetrating black eyes "...play tennis, I'm in a very dangerous position on the other side of a bargaining table from you."

Her nipples tingled at the suggestion in his voice and she stretched, trying to look casual. "I only want what's fair."

"I suppose there is the matter of the cookbook." He stared at the ground for a moment, then met her gaze again.

"Is that the red leather book I found in Mom's kitchen?" She thought of those carefully written creamy pages with their lovely drawings.

A line appeared between Naldo's brows. "Yes. That's the one. My father illustrated it." He looked up, gazing into the trees behind her. "He always liked to draw."

Oh. So that's why she didn't remember her mom being artistic. The book was a joint effort. A labor of love. The image of them working on it together made her bite her lip to stem a surge of emotion.

"I can't picture your father drawing. I always saw him in action, striding about the place." It was hard to imagine the dynamic Robert De Leon taking the time and care to make those intricate and carefully observed illustrations.

"Oh, yeah. He painted, too. Usually early in the morning, before the day got rolling. He loved to go out to the orchards with an easel and capture the trees in bloom."

An orange blossom petal drifted down from the tree above them and landed on Anna's belly. "I don't think there's a more beautiful sight on earth," she murmured, looking up at the white clustered branches.

"There isn't." Naldo looked at her. "I've traveled enough to know that. This is heaven, right here. My dad knew he lived in paradise and he lived every minute of it to the fullest."

Anna chewed her lip. She'd once been so keen to get away, to get on with building a "real life." Real life had turned out to be a crushing disappointment compared to life here in Paradiso.

"What's the matter?" Naldo brushed a strand of hair off her face.

"I didn't realize how much I'd missed this place."

"It seeps into your blood, doesn't it?" He stroked her cheek with his thumb. "Wraps itself around you, and doesn't want to let you go. I guess that's why the De Leons have been here so damn long."

And why I don't want to leave again.

Overcome by a wave of panic, Anna shook her head, tossing her hair. Naldo pulled his hand back.

You have to leave. You have no choice. This isn't your home anymore.

"I guess that's why I can't stomach the idea of parting with even one acre." Naldo's dimple appeared. His words, spoken so casually, made her gut twist with anguish. A simple reminder that he wanted her to take the money and give *his* land back.

She sat up and reached for her dress, trying to maintain a veneer of calm. *Think business.* "I still don't understand why the cookbook was mentioned in the will. Because they did it together?"

"It's not the book that's important, so much as the recipes. I guess he wanted to acknowledge that they were your mom's." Naldo shifted onto his elbow, frowning at the dress in her hand. "They're the foundation of the retail business."

She froze. "The marinades and dressings that you sell in supermarkets?"

"Yes."

"The products that netted three million dollars in profits in their first year of production?" Her thoughts, spoken aloud, made that now familiar furrow reappear between Naldo's brows.

"Your mother developed the recipes as an employee of the estate." His tone had turned professional. Cold.

"Of course." A surge of fresh hurt mingled with fury and

stung her. "She came up with ideas that generate millions in cash for the estate, while earning a cook's salary."

"She was compensated in other ways."

"The jewels." Anna's blood chilled. "Your father bought her off. Kept her quiet."

Naldo blew out an exasperated burst of air and sat up. "What happened to you, Anna? What made you so bitter and untrusting? My father *loved* your mother. They were a team—much as it pains me to say it—and they did almost everything together. He gave her *an acre of the estate*, for crying out loud. Do you have any idea how extraordinary that is? It's never happened before in the history of the De Leon family."

"The estate. That's all it comes down to, isn't it? Preserving the estate, building the estate, growing the profits. The idea of that one acre not being under your control is a real burr under your saddle isn't it? Did Ricky tell you I didn't want the acre mowed?"

Naldo raised an eyebrow. "Yes, he told me. Why don't you want it mowed? Are you raising hay? Or just raising hell?"

This woman was crazy, no doubt about it. She knelt across from him on the sand with her dress fisted in her lap. Light and shade filtered through the blossom-covered tree and made tracery patterns on her stunning, slender body.

Her bright eyes shone with the fire of her passion. Anna Marcus was passionate in every possible way.

He hid a smile that wanted to sneak across his mouth. Yes, he wanted his acre back, and he'd get it, but not without going through that fire some more. Lucky thing he didn't burn easily.

"Just making sure we all know where we stand." On her

own cue, she stood and shook out her dress. "I think you should bring the gems back to the cottage."

A swell of naked lust rolled through him at the sight of those long legs that wrapped around him so perfectly, climbing back into the white cotton dress.

"Need help with the zipper?" He didn't try to hide the evidence of his arousal.

"I've got it." She zipped up the back without a hitch.

"You would. You don't need anyone, do you? No wonder marriage didn't suit you."

That stopped her in her tracks. She shoved a lock of hair awkwardly off her face. "You don't know anything about my marriage."

"No. I don't. Anything I should know?"

Damn. On the one hand, he was curious. On the other, he didn't want to know anything *at all* about Anna and another man. He shifted in the sand, uncomfortable.

"He left me." She said it quickly, and for once her fire seemed to dim. "I guess you're right. He left me for someone totally different. Said he wanted someone quiet and nurturing. More submissive."

"I'm sorry." The hurt in her eyes tore at his chest. "He was the wrong man for you, because you sure aren't cut out to be submissive."

"I guess, like you said, marriage doesn't suit me."

"Hey." He reached for his pants. "Don't let a bad experience get you down. You just need someone who appreciates you for who you are."

"I don't think there's anyone that crazy." She tried to sound lighthearted, but it didn't fool him.

"You're a woman in a million."

"Yeah?" She tossed her hair and narrowed her eyes. "Is that why you're willing to pay four million to get rid of me?"

He couldn't help laughing. She was right, of course.

At this point he was offering her far more than what the gems, the cookbook and the land were worth. What would it take to make this woman see sense?

It might help if he could keep his damn hands off her for a whole day.

Why was he making love to the daughter of his father's lover? She was the last woman on earth he should be interested in.

He shook his head. Anna Marcus was definitely having a disturbing effect on him. He'd actually experienced a surge of relief that the jewels were legally hers, otherwise he'd have felt like he was cheating her out of them. And the cookbook, too. He'd originally intended to gloss over that, to have her leave without knowing what the clause in the will really meant.

But he couldn't do it.

Since he'd gotten to know her again he had a powerful urge to protect her interests and safeguard her rights, even at the expense of the estate—not to mention his own sanity.

No doubt it was just his sense of honor. His father had raised him to do the right thing.

She slipped her feet back into her sandals. Pink soles peeped at him for a tantalizing second as she put them on, before he dragged his eyes away.

He needed to back off and play it cool. The more he came on strong, the more she fought him.

The worst part was how much he enjoyed that. Anna's fire lit an inferno inside him in a way he'd never experienced with any other woman. He loved the way she stood up to him. That she didn't fawn and simper and pander over him like so many women who saw him as some kind of trophy, not as a man.

Anna saw him as a man, all right.

And despite his duty to the estate, he couldn't help seeing her as a woman. A savvy businesswoman who refused to be cheated, a loyal and caring woman who wanted to see her mother's memory honored, a passionate and sensual woman who called to something stronger than principle and pragmatism.

He could tell she loved the estate, too, that she felt a deep connection to land and the trees.

He snapped his attention away from the hot burst of feeling rushing through his chest.

It was time to be practical. "I'll send Tom over with the gems when I get back. Then the ball is in your court." He settled back in the sand with his hands behind his head, trying to look like he didn't care much one way or the other.

"Good." She shot him a dirty look that only tickled his libido.

As she stalked back down the row of trees in her unsuitable shoes, he heaved a deep sigh, which brought him no relaxation whatsoever.

He just wanted to put things back the way they should be. The estate whole and entire. The family secrets buried safely where they belonged.

Why did it have to be so hard?

If he didn't get rid of Anna soon, rumors really would start to fly, and once they got out there'd be no putting that genie back in the bottle. He should be doing everything in his power to make her leave—right now.

Instead, all he wanted to do was run his hands over her silky skin and trace the proud angle of her chin with kisses. To make bone-shaking, earth-tilting love to her again.

And again.

He scrubbed a hand over his face, inadvertently getting a bunch of gritty sand on it. He had sand all over him from head to toe and was lying naked and alone in his own orange grove.

What was wrong with this picture?

Relax. It's a fair offer. More than fair. She'll come to her senses, take the money, and go.

The thought made him more uncomfortable than ever.

Eight

The sound of footsteps on the cottage steps roused Anna from a deep night's sleep. Not really footsteps, more like loud thuds. She sat up, heart pounding.

"Who's there?"

She squinted against morning sunlight as the bedroom door flung open.

Who else?

Naldo stood in the doorway, fury hot in his eyes. He brandished a tabloid-size newspaper. "What do you mean by this?"

"Get out of my room!" She clutched the covers around herself, more out of instinctive self-defense than modesty.

"I'm not going anywhere until you explain this article."

"I have no idea what you're talking about."

He flung the paper down on the rumpled bedcover and rapped the page with the back of his hand. "You know exactly what I'm talking about."

Still sleepy, she squinted, then rubbed her eyes, trying to focus on the tiny newsprint. *De Leon Heir in Legal Wrangle* was the rather small heading of a short article on page eight.

She picked up the paper and held it closer.

An intriguing wrinkle appeared in the long and illustrious history of the De Leon family, when the late Robert De Leon left a small tract of estate land to an employee. As the De Leons have clung to every acre they own since the 1500s, this has raised eyebrows all over the county. An inside source confirmed that Robert De Leon's long-rumored affair was in fact with this employee, forty-eight-year-old Leticia Marcus, who worked on the estate as a cook for fifteen years before her recent death in an automobile accident.

Anna bit her lip as fresh grief flooded her.

The situation might be further complicated by the estate's recent venture into the retail market. Some say the late Ms. Marcus was the mastermind behind the award-winning products that are seeing strong sales across the nation. Ms. Marcus's daughter has been in town for several days, and seems to have no immediate plans to relinquish her claims on the estate. Is the great De Leon empire under siege?

She realized her jaw had fallen open, and she snapped it shut.

"Why did you do this?" Naldo leaned over her, his voice low and menacing.

"Do what?" she rasped. "I had nothing to do with this."

"It had to be you. You're the only person with 'insider information'."

Anna blinked. Naldo De Leon was in her bedroom—uninvited—accusing her of spreading libelous rumors. He hadn't even asked, he *assumed* she was the source. White-hot rage streaked along her nerves. Did this man's arrogance have no limits?

"You said you'd like to tell the papers what kind of man my father really was." His low voice joined his eyes in an aggressive confrontation that wreaked havoc on her stubborn streak.

She let go of the covers and crossed her arms over her chest. "What if I did give them the information?"

Naldo's brows lowered. "Do you have any idea what this means?"

"Sure. People will know the *truth*. It is the truth, remember?"

"It is private, proprietary information about my father's personal life. The De Leon name appears in the paper only for announcements of births, marriages and deaths, not on the gossip pages."

He straightened his shoulders and lifted his chin.

Anna exploded into a chuckle. Yes. His arrogance really did have no limits. "Oh, come on. There must have been articles about the new line of products."

"Yes. Of course. But a public relations firm in New York handles those. Naturally your mother's name was never mentioned in connection with them."

"Naturally," she returned sarcastically. "Perhaps you can call them in to 'handle' this too?" She smiled sweetly.

Naldo inhaled deeply, obviously using every last ounce of self-control not to take her by the shoulders and shake her. "So you admit it?"

"I don't admit a thing."

She could see Naldo's powerful chest heaving under his dark shirt. Any minute now, steam was going to start rising out of his artfully tousled black hair. "You are impossible."

"Me? You're the one who's broken into my house and marched into my bedroom uninvited! I'm in my pajamas, for crying out loud." She indicated her pink cami. "If anyone is 'under siege,' it's me. Could you maybe show a little common politeness for a change?"

Naldo blinked. She saw his Adam's apple move, then he drew himself up to his full height and nodded brusquely. "You're right. I should have knocked. But I want a full explanation of this. The De Leon family does not take scandal lying down, of that you can be sure."

His dark gaze trapped her focus for several intense seconds. A heady mix of unreadable thoughts and emotions seemed to swirl in those dark, penetrating eyes, and in her mind. Then he turned and left.

She collapsed back against the pillow, heart thumping.

A full explanation? She didn't have one, but she was going to get one. She heard his car engine with relief. At least he wasn't waiting for his explanation at the bottom of the stairs.

Naldo had left the newspaper lying on the bed. *The Sunshine Post.* She remembered the local paper her mother used to look for yard sale announcements in. Hardly the *National Enquirer*, but she could see that this was a nice juicy local tidbit. And it was true.

But no way would she let Naldo blame her for planting it. She'd find out who did this, and the best way to start was simply to ask.

"My source is confidential." The classic line was spoken not by an old-time visor-and-vest-wearing hack, but by a pimply youth dressed like a skateboarder.

Anna and *Sunshine Post* reporter Thomas Craig carried their iced teas to an outdoor table at the Bon Appétit café on Main Street in the middle of a glorious, sunny spring morning.

"How do you know her information was accurate?"

"It checked out."

"Ah, so it *was* a female?" Anna raised her eyebrows and took a sip of iced tea.

He tilted his head and winked. "I'm sure we can find some information to trade with each other. You're Leticia Marcus's daughter?"

"Yes. Everyone calls her Letty. Called her Letty, I guess I'm still not used to—"

"How long had she been involved with Robert De Leon?" He leaned forward to sip from his straw and his dirty blond hair hung in his eyes. No doubt hiding a gleam of voracious curiosity.

"I have no idea if they even did have an affair." Her knee-jerk response surprised her. She had no doubt they'd been lovers. Even Naldo admitted it. So why was she prevaricating now?

"Oh, come on." Craig's wide mouth tilted in a mocking smile. "Everyone in town knows they had a long-term affair."

"They were both private people," she said stiffly. "I hardly think they'd have let everyone in town in on their business."

"So, you admit there was 'business,' as you so tactfully put it?" He sipped his iced tea through the straw again. A skull-and-crossbones ring glinted on one of his fingers.

"I admit nothing of the kind."

He snorted. "Come on, we're all adults here. And now you're getting into it with Naldo."

"What?" Her eyes snapped open. A flush started to

creep up from the neckline of her T-shirt. Ugh! If he didn't suspect anything already, he would now.

"Over the land. He wants you to sell, but you won't."

"Of course I will. I don't want that land."

"So why haven't you sold and left yet?"

"I have to sort through my mother's things."

"And rekindle an old flame, perhaps?" He cocked his head, letting his long hair flop aside to reveal green eyes glinting with...malice?

"There's nothing between me and Naldo." The bare-faced lie made her revealing flush deepen.

"Why do I *not* believe you?" He winked.

She inhaled sharply. "I grew up here. Naldo was away at boarding school most of the time, so I saw him when he was home for vacations. Naldo and I both loved sports, so, sure, we spent some time fooling around on the tennis court and shooting hoops. That's all there was to it. We weren't really friends, even. He didn't recognize me when I came back." This time the truth gave her a nasty, nagging sensation.

"And now you're all grown up, both single..." He took another sip and peered at her through his hair.

"I'm not single, I'm divorced," she sputtered.

He smiled, revealing straight, white teeth. "Last time I checked, divorced meant single."

"As you've so astutely observed, Naldo and I are both adults. What we do is our own business. As it happens, we are simply negotiating a price for the property left to my mother. When we've reached an agreement I will sell and leave. Simple as that." She sipped her iced tea, trying to keep her temper in check.

"Your mother developed the recipes that are minting money for the family?"

"I believe she did."

"Then I bet you want a piece of that juicy pie." Craig leaned forward and lifted a skinny brow.

"I certainly do not. My mother developed those recipes as an employee of the estate." She clamped her lips together, hardly able to believe she was making the same argument Naldo had made.

"She must have been a pretty devoted employee. The De Leons are famous for being one of the best employers anywhere. The staff are like family, no?"

"Absolutely. That's why they keep the same people for so long."

"And I guess that's how Robert De Leon kept his affair with your mother a secret for so many years. No one wanted to risk their comfy perch by blowing the lid off the chicken coop."

"Blowing the lid off? Please. You're acting like there's an actual story here. Who cares what Robert De Leon was doing in his spare time? Why on earth is that anyone's business but his?"

The cool, sweet, iced tea did nothing to extinguish her simmering indignation. She'd like to crush this snotty little jerk under her sandal.

Why are you defending Robert De Leon? He treated your mother as a mistress. He could have married her, but he didn't.

"Come on. We both know they had an affair."

"My mother would have told me, and she never said a word."

That still hurt. But it confirmed that her mother wanted to keep her love life a secret, and it was Anna's duty to respect that.

"And now you and Naldo are continuing the legacy.

A legacy of *passion*." The green eyes narrowed to vicious slits.

Anna narrowly resisted the urge to throw her iced tea at him. "Naldo and I are working out some business matters. Why don't you go write about something that actually matters? Isabela De Leon came to you with this, didn't she?"

"I cannot confirm, or deny…" He winked at her.

"I thought so." She slammed some money down on the table, annoyed that she had to pay for him since she'd invited him. At least she had the information she was looking for, not that she hadn't known it from the start. "Thanks for your time," she muttered. Then she marched off down the street, bristling with irritation at the reporter, Isabela, Naldo and anyone else who wanted to make her life more of a mess than it already was.

She wasn't sure if Isabela had hinted at an affair between her and Naldo, or if she'd given that information herself with her guilty blushes. This meeting was probably *not* a good idea, but at least she'd learned that Isabela was the source.

She'd been sure Isabela had planted the article, but why would she want to have the family scandals blabbed all over town? Did she want to hurt Naldo? Was it part of her plan to force him to sell the estate?

Anger simmered inside her at the idea that Naldo's own sister was trying to undermine the estate.

But why should she care? It wasn't as if Naldo *meant* something to her.

If anything, he deserved it.

Naldo never came back to get her news about the true source of the article. When she stopped by the house to tell him it was his sister who'd gone to the papers, she learned he'd gone to a polo match near Ocala. Right now he was probably out partying, with an heiress on each arm.

Tom had delivered the gems to her the previous evening and stored them back in the dark attic as she requested. He gave her a wary look along with his polite greeting when she said "hi" to him at the house. Even the usually cheery Pilar seemed cool.

Back at the cottage, she folded up a white cotton sweater of her mother's and put it in yet another pile to go in the van. Why couldn't she seem to throw anything away? What was she going to do with all this stuff? Maybe being adrift and rootless, with no idea what the future held, was turning her into a pack rat, clutching at anything that might bring a sense of security.

She slept a while, then got up to pack just as light was breaking over the horizon. She turned the air conditioner off—why not enjoy the balmy Florida heat while she still could? It was probably fifty degrees in Boston right now.

Without the whirring of the A/C, the chirping and warbling of thousands of birds began to fill her ears. She'd never paid much attention to birds while she lived here. She took their gentle morning wake-up song for granted, along with the rich scented air and the warm, year-round sun.

Since then she'd lived so long surrounded by the roar of traffic and the *whup-whup* of early morning sirens, that she had a burning curiosity to see what kinds of birds were making that pretty music.

She shoved up the old sash window.

Wow. There was that air again. So much of it, fresh and clean and clear and perfumed with oranges. She inhaled deeply, letting it fill her lungs and send its invigorating, scented oxygen zipping into her bloodstream.

Leaving the first time had been easy. Leaving again—for good—was going to be a whole different story.

The sound of an engine growling close by made her crane her neck around to the front of the house. She'd taken to parking her van on the grass in case anyone needed access to the polo arena. Who ever heard of a private polo arena? She shook her head.

The engine stopped and she heard a door slam.

Great. Yet another opportunity for Naldo to catch her in her jammies. She grabbed a sky blue dress, another one of her mother's, off the hanger in the closet, and was still switching it for her pajamas when she heard the loud knock.

"Coming!"

She shimmied into the pretty summer dress, sure that at any second the door would fling open to admit her impatient and imperious guest.

But it didn't. Frowning, she slid on some sandals and hurried downstairs.

Naldo was actually waiting outside the door?

She opened up. Sure enough, it was him. Resplendent in perfectly pressed khakis and a white shirt. "To what do I owe this not entirely unexpected pleasure?" She gestured for him to enter.

He gave her a look so strange that she almost tripped on the threshold.

Hurt. That's what she saw in his eyes.

Not the flashing glints of anger she'd grown quite used to, but something deeper, darker and possibly far more dangerous.

He took a step into the kitchen, unfurled a paper that he'd carried under his arm and laid it on the table.

"You already showed me the article," she said softly. He still hadn't spoken.

"Read it."

She picked up the paper.

Legacy of Passion. The front-page headline punched her in the gut and stole her breath. The paper crinkled as her fists tightened around it.

Daughter of De Leon employee continues tradition: Affair with the Boss.

Her heart stopped. Or at least that's what it felt like. She looked up at Naldo. "Wha—?"

"Keep reading."

> A conversation with Anna Marcus, daughter of De Leon estate employee Leticia Marcus, sheds fresh light on the legal skirmish over estate land reported in yesterday's paper. Ms. Marcus, pretty, blond and twenty-six, is back in town to handle her mother's affairs—and to have one of her own.

"This is complete nonsense," she spat.

"Really? He heard it from you." Naldo looked at her coolly.

"No way. He totally made this up. It's crazy." Her heart thudded.

"Oh, is it? Now you seem to be the one who has a problem with the truth."

"I would hardly say we're having an affair." The newsprint blurred and jumbled before her eyes. She had no idea what she and Naldo were having. Or weren't having. Her throat tightened.

"Exactly what would you call it? And how do you explain the quotes?"

"What quotes?"

"Read on."

She and Naldo have a passionate past. "Sure, we spent some time fooling around," admits the bold and spunky Ms. Marcus. "Naldo and I are both adults. What we do is our own business."

"That was quoted completely out of context!" Her hand flew to her mouth and the paper sagged in the other.

"So you admit you did talk to him?"

"I did, but only because I wanted to find out who planted the seeds for the other article. It was Isabela."

"He said that?"

"Well, not in so many words…." She trailed off. That pimply punk had *used* her.

"Fooling around?" A bitter laugh shook Naldo.

"I was talking about how we used to fool around on the courts. I can't believe he managed to make it sound so…so…"

"Sexual?" Naldo's steady black gaze challenged her. She swallowed.

"Don't stop reading now. It's just about to get good. In fact, I'll read it." He seized the paper and read aloud.

"'Ms. Marcus has good reason to seek a little tenderness in the arms of a former lover. In the last year she has divorced her husband of five years and declared *bankruptcy*.'"

She gasped. His emphasis on the final word made it hang in the air. Naldo stared at her for an agonizing moment, then focused his eyes back on the paper. "'The commercial real estate firm Ms. Marcus owned with her husband, Barry Lennox, went belly up after a string of risky investments, and the Marcus-Lennox marriage went south along with it.'

"'Flat broke and newly divorced from a man who has since remarried, Ms. Marcus found herself once again within arm's reach of one of Florida's wealthiest and most powerful men, citrus heir Reynaldo De Leon'." He glared at her with narrowed eyes and her stomach clenched like a fist.

"'Reynaldo De Leon and Anna Marcus have wasted no time rekindling their old flame, following in the footsteps of their late parents, Robert De Leon and his longtime cook, Leticia Marcus.'"

He paused and stared at her for a long time with an intensity that made her shiver. Then he read on.

"'Whispers still echo around the local corridors of power that the death of the late Mrs. DeLeon was no accident. It's long been rumored that news of Robert De Leon's affair with his cook caused his wife to *take her own life*.'" He emphasized the last words with grim finality.

"Oh, my god." Anna's hand flew to her mouth. Her head started pounding. "Is this true?"

"Yes." Naldo hurled the word at her. "It's true. She swallowed a bottle of painkillers. I found her in her bedroom." His eyes glittered with pain. "I tried to revive her, but she was already gone."

"Oh, no." She murmured it into her hand as blood pounded in her brain. "The affair began while she was still alive?"

Naldo stared at her, his face suddenly hard as stone. "Yes. And my mother knew. She couldn't live with the shame of it."

Anna sank into a kitchen chair. Her own father had been a married man, but her mom swore she didn't know about his wife until after she became pregnant and told him.

Here she'd apparently entered knowingly into an affair with a married man.

And it had killed his wife. "I'm so, so sorry."

"Why? It had nothing to do with you. But you can see

why my dad would do *anything* to keep the story from coming out. He bought and paid for a decade of silence." Naldo paused, holding her gaze with a fierce stare. "Now he's dead, and the silence has been broken."

Anna sagged into her chair, hardly able to believe what she'd just heard. It was tempting to judge, but she could see why her mother—alone and struggling for so many years—would seek affection in the arms of her strong, charming and charismatic employer.

Now she knew why her mom never told her. She almost wished she'd never found out about the affair. Maybe some things were better kept secret.

"You didn't tell me you were *bankrupt*." His harsh words scattered her thoughts.

"I..." A pink tide of humiliation flooded her brain. She'd almost forgotten that tidbit of information after the horrifying revelation of the suicide. Now Naldo knew she was a failure.

If only the scuffed linoleum floor would open up and swallow her whole.

"I thought you were toying with me because you didn't need the money. That it was some kind of game to you. Now I know you're broke, I don't know whether your continued refusal to accept my offer is motivated by greed or insanity?"

"It's true. I am broke." The words, spoken aloud, lifted some of the weight off her chest.

"I know. I called the publisher as soon as I saw this. Then I woke the reporter up at home. Once he stopped stammering, he told me how easy it was to do some Google-ing and make a few phone calls to Boston." His gaze was unreadable, but still contained no traces of the fury she might have expected.

She let out a sigh. "I didn't want you to find out."

His eyes softened. "I know."

"You're not angry?"

"Not about you being poor." A smile tugged at his mouth. "Sure, I was a little steamed when I found out you'd deceived me. But you're a proud woman, and you didn't want my pity. I respect that."

A funny feeling tugged at the pit of Anna's stomach. Why wasn't he mad? That she could deal with. This casual attitude threw her right off balance.

"I didn't say any of that stuff about you and me."

"The reporter told me he quoted you word for word." He raised a dark brow.

"Out of context! The part about a relationship between us is total speculation on his part. You could just deny it."

"Oh, could I? *It's true, isn't it?* To quote a hotheaded and high-strung woman of my acquaintance."

"I am not high-strung!"

"I notice you're not arguing on the hotheaded." The hard line of his mouth tilted into a half smile.

"No." She bit her lower lip. "I don't think I could argue with that. I'm sorry I let that journalist use me. I fell into a trap. I should have known better. I'm so embarrassed that everyone will know I'm a big failure. I never even told my mom. She was so proud of me."

She bit the inside of her mouth. No tears came, though. She must be getting used to body blows of disappointment and humiliation.

"Your husband remarried already?" Naldo spoke quietly.

"He was seeing her while we were married. I didn't know. Too busy working." She pushed the words between tight lips. "I also didn't know he was forging my signature and using our assets as collateral to buy more properties without asking me. When the bottom fell out of the market we were wiped out and owed a lot of money. We had no choice but to declare bankruptcy."

"I'm sorry."

"Don't be. You're right, I don't want your pity."

"You don't want my money, either, do you?" A furrow appeared between his brows.

"No. I don't. I only wish I didn't need it so badly."

"There's no shame in taking what's rightfully owed you."

"Sure there is. I don't believe in gaining success through inherited wealth. I prefer to earn it."

Naldo considered this. A twinkle appeared in his eye. "Are you implying that I'm sponging off my ancestors?"

"You said it, not me." She cocked her head.

The odd expression on his face, like he was actually contemplating whether what she said was true, touched something tender inside her. "No, I don't mean that. I saw you out there planting that tree like it really mattered, and I know from my mom's letters that you work harder than anyone on the estate."

He looked at her, serious. "We're all partners in this endeavor."

"Partners in more ways than one, sometimes."

It took a moment to sink in. "Indeed."

She took a deep breath. "I'm sure the story about us will blow over as soon as I'm gone. I bet you can't wait to be rid of me." Her voice sounded flat, which was exactly how she felt.

Naldo shot her a shimmering black gaze that made her stomach quiver.

"You're wrong. I want you to stay."

Nine

"For what possible reason could you want me to stay?" Anna blinked rapidly, trying to figure out what Naldo was up to.

"I don't want our affair to end." His deep voice thrummed with assurance.

"The affair that's causing a scandal in the local paper?"

Good humor shone in his eyes. "Exactly."

"But I don't understand. I thought you hated gossip and innuendo."

"I do. But there are other things I'd hate more, like not getting to challenge you to a *real* tennis match. Or not getting to kiss your lips into silence again." A smile tugged his dimple into existence.

No kisses required. Her lips had been stunned into silence.

When she found her voice again, she was frowning.

"But aren't I a reminder to everyone that your father had an affair with my mother?"

"I suppose you are." The dimple stayed firm.

Anna's thoughts ducked and dived like barn swallows. *Is he falling in love with me?*

"I don't really understand what you're saying. You think I should keep the cottage and live in it?"

"Oh, no." His expression turned more serious. "You can get a far more comfortable house in town. A new villa with a pool, perhaps? This place is old and cramped."

Or was this some new trick to get her to sell out?

"My mom loved this cottage."

"I know. My father tried to persuade her to move into a larger place, but she wouldn't hear of it. Some people are just stubborn, I guess." His eyes twinkled.

Stubborn? Try confused. Or afraid. What was he trying to pull?

He picked up her hand, and his warm skin made her fingers tingle. He brought them to his lips, and kissed them. Those firm, sensuous lips, with their arrogant tilt, sent a shiver of desire rushing through her.

"I like having you here." He held her finger close to his lips, and she could feel his warm breath on her skin. His words stole into her consciousness and crept toward her heart.

How many times had she dreamed of hearing Naldo De Leon say he wanted her?

"But don't you care about what people will say?"

"No." The intensity of his black gaze stole her breath. A glance at the determined set of his lips gave her a rash urge to kiss them.

She resisted.

"Why not? I thought you—"

"I have more important things to concern myself with."

Her lips parted as his eyes drifted down over her face. She felt her cheeks heat. He lowered his face to hers, giving her time to notice the heat of his skin, time to inhale his subtle musky scent.

Their lips came together slowly. It happened by imperceptible degrees, but the impact of skin touching skin slammed her like a car wreck. Suddenly her hands were on him, clutching at his shirt, her fingers pushing up into his hair.

His arms closed around her, holding her tight, squeezing her with a passion that made her breath catch as he kissed her with a ferocity she could never have imagined.

I love you, Naldo De Leon.

The thought never seemed to be far from her mind lately. His firm, warm embrace filled her with a surge of excitement and a shocking sense of well-being. It felt *right*.

But how could it be?

He wasn't asking her to move in with him. He wasn't asking her to marry him.

She pulled back, a painful effort that involved tearing her lips from his impassioned kiss against the urging of every cell in her body.

"You want to have an affair with me." Her words emerged breathless. Her lips stung, still quivering with the force of his kiss.

Naldo's narrowed eyes burned with naked lust. He blinked once, then lowered his lips over hers again, in wordless assent to her question.

She succumbed to the sensual heat of the moment, drifting in his arms, until her eyes snapped open and she pulled back again.

A pang of pain stung her heart. Naldo would never marry her. She was no pedigreed Spanish contessa. She was the illegitimate daughter of a cook and she'd never fit into Naldo's world of three-hundred-year-old porcelain plates and four-hundred-year-old prejudices.

Sure, he wanted her. He wanted to kiss her and lick her and rub his impatient hands over her fevered skin. To strip her naked and make love to her until they both lay breathless and exhausted.

Her body ached with the desire to do those things with him, preferably *right now,* but her mind whispered warnings that made far too much sense.

He'll use you. He'll get what he wants, take his fill, then move on. And where will that leave you?

"I don't want to be a rich man's mistress."

"You wouldn't be a rich man's mistress." Naldo's husky voice filled her ears.

Did he plan to ask her to be his wife?

"You'd be a rich man's *girlfriend.*"

Naldo took hold of her chin with his thumb and forefinger. He tilted her face to look up at his. "And if you take my offer, you'll be a rich man's *rich* girlfriend."

Humor still sparkled in his eyes. So confident. As if it didn't occur to him that she would say no.

"Four million dollars. It's yours. All you have to do is say the word."

A shudder of powerful emotion rocked her, stinging her fingers and toes.

Love?

Fear?

Or both, shaken into a cocktail that threatened to deprive her of her senses.

"I can feel your heart beating." Naldo placed two long, powerful fingers on the pulse at her neck. His chest pressed against hers, their hearts pounding together.

Her lips itched to touch his. To settle into the firm warmth of his kiss. To shun words that tangled into confusion as she tried to make sense of a situation that seemed so…impossible.

Too good to be true?

"I want to make love to you." Naldo's harsh whisper tickled her ear. Heat rippled through her, sparking a fire low in her belly.

His fingers slid down to cup her buttocks and caress them, through the smooth fabric of her dress.

Her breathing came quicker as her nipples tightened against his chest.

I want to love you.

Her stray thought was different from what he offered. One, a phrase implying something physical, transient, the other bringing with it the promise of a connection that could last a lifetime.

She swallowed hard.

His fingers slid around her leg, and sneaked up the sensitive skin of her inner thigh. Her sex responded with a welcoming throb.

"Stop, please." She forced the words from quivering lips. She squeezed her eyes shut, trying to get a grip on all the sensations taking her body by storm.

Naldo's broad hand paused on her thigh. Her skin hummed beneath his fingers.

"You know you want to." His deep voice wrapped itself around her, thick with temptation.

"I need time to think," she managed. She wriggled, trying to free herself from his firm embrace, even though it was the last thing she truly wanted.

"You think far too much." Naldo softened his grip. His gleaming black eyes met hers and he pushed a stray strand of hair off her forehead. "Too much thinking can confuse you. Sometimes you just have to act."

"It's all so sudden. One minute you're desperate to get rid of me, throwing money at me and trying to make me disappear. Now you want me to stay? It doesn't make sense."

She still couldn't get over the nagging suspicion that this was all part of his plan to reclaim the land and the jewels.

"Trust me, I've done everything in my power to make myself see sense." Naldo tilted his proud head. "I've told myself time and again that it's better for the family and the estate if you leave. I know that. As heir to the estate I should settle down into a 'sensible' marriage. But I don't want to, I want *you*."

The passion in his words tugged at something deep inside her. But the words themselves stung like a hard slap.

She was right.

He would never marry her.

It didn't even occur to him that she might be offended by him saying it out loud. Obviously the idea was so impossible that it didn't even bear consideration.

She pulled out of his arms and flew across the room, her breath coming in gulps. She took a deep breath. Common sense for her was taking what he offered. Four million dollars. As Isabela had said, the offer might not last.

Naldo looked at her steadily. "If you like, you could still live in the cottage. I know it means a lot to you."

His words made her bite her lip. The offer was a big sacrifice for him. Tongues would wag like crazy. *The boss visiting the servants' quarters in time-honored tradition.* But the prospect of being able to live here among the groves, in Paradiso, quickened her pulse.

And if he could make the rash step of giving in to his lust for her, maybe one day he might take an even rasher step....

But what if he didn't?

What if he used her the way two men had used her mother? Without ever promising marriage, or any commitment beyond an evening of pleasure.

It would break her heart.

"I think you should leave now." She said it softly. She didn't want him to leave at all. She wanted him to stay, forever. To hold her in his arms and promise her all those things that hadn't even crossed his mind. That probably never would.

Naldo reached into his back pocket. "Here's the revised contract. Just so you know I mean what I say." He placed the slim envelope on the table.

He parted with a brief kiss that left her lips humming and her mind spinning. She sank into a chair at the kitchen table as his engine purred down the drive.

She could have it all. More money than she could have imagined, Naldo, and glorious days living here in the most beautiful place on earth.

But for how long?

The cottage and the land were a place to call home. Should she take cold cash for a gift her mother might have wanted her to cherish and protect for a lifetime?

And what about the recipes? Perhaps she should investigate what legal rights she might be able to secure in her mother's name?

No. Her mom created those recipes for the estate, the place she loved and the people she loved. She must have been thrilled to contribute to their prosperity in such a tangible way.

She picked up the beautiful book and leafed through the

pages that shone with love and care. The delicate line drawings revealed such a different side to the gruff land-owner she remembered, the man who'd made her mother happy.

And now that she thought about it, maybe her mother had tried to tell her about her late-in-life love. Snatches of fond conversation, chivalrous visits from "the boss," the new grove of trees, a new light in her mom's eyes...

And dismissive teenaged put-downs from Anna's own lips. The voice of insecurity and unease drawing a sharp line between her tiny family and the mighty De Leons who employed them.

Her mother had decided to keep quiet about the love of her life, perhaps not wanting her own relationship, which began as adultery, held up to the harsh light of Anna's exacting standards.

She bit her knuckle hard, trying not to cry. *All or nothing, that's you, Anna. You have to have it all, or you don't want any of it.* She was no different from Naldo. Wanting everything black and white, with no gray areas.

She wanted marriage, a lifetime of love, a real family where her children had a mother and a father.

Her mom was probably right to keep quiet about her affair with Robert De Leon. She would have poked and prodded and pried. She would have asked, "Why won't he marry you?" She wouldn't have understood.

She could understand now, though, after the dismal failure of her own marriage.

True love is not so easy to find.

Her mom must have accepted that Robert De Leon would never marry her. She must have woven that accep-tance into the fabric of her life with the quiet strength she'd used to weather so much adversity.

She stood and closed the book.

Could she do the same thing with Naldo? Learn to accept that life wasn't black and white, all or nothing? Love this proud and demanding man, even though he would likely never want to make her his wife and partner?

Could she? She bit her lip hard. *Probably not.*

Anna came back from town with groceries to cook herself a real dinner. She'd pulled the van up close to the house, with the plan to unpack her belongings from it tomorrow.

She was about to sit down to a salad of chicken, Asian noodles, and fresh orange segments from the Summer's Shadow grove, when she heard a car pull up outside. A glance out the window curdled her appetite.

Isabela.

She was up and at the door before Isabela had a chance to knock. "I'm just sitting down to dinner. What is it?"

Isabela didn't remove her dark glasses despite the setting sun. "Naldo told me you still haven't sold to him." Anna heard emotion in her voice and wondered if it was real or fake. "What are you trying to do? Don't you know that every day you stay here prolongs the scandal?"

"You've got some nerve talking about scandal when *you* planted that story in the paper." Anna stepped through the doorway, intentionally crowding the chiffon-clad diva.

"I thought I could convince Naldo to sell. That whispers and rumors would make him want to leave. I never intended for them to know that *my brother* was fooling around with the cook's *daughter*. Obviously neither you nor he has any shame. What if the European paparazzi gets hold of this?"

Her voice shook. Her big, black glasses hid her eyes, and Anna could only guess at the fury behind the reflective surface.

She couldn't help laughing. "You are kidding! Why on earth would the European paparazzi care about what's going on in a sleepy little Florida town?

"I wouldn't expect someone like you to understand." Isabela's lips puckered into a moue of distaste. "The De Leons are one of the oldest families in Europe, and everything we do is of interest."

In your dreams. Anna crossed her arms and congratulated herself on holding her tongue.

"I have a name in the arts," Isabela spat. Chiffon ruffles fluttered as she gestured with a plump pale hand. "I'll be a laughingstock."

Anna choked back the laughter bubbling up inside her. No sense insulting Naldo's sister if she could help it. She was his family after all and Naldo was big on family. "I hardly see how, but perhaps you should go back to Paris immediately and try to save your reputation. If you don't mind, I have dinner to eat."

"Listen to me." Finally the glasses came off. Beady black eyes seized Anna's attention. "If you don't leave, *now*, you'll destroy Naldo the way your mother destroyed our family. You're casting some kind of sick spell over him, just like your mother did with our father. He's lost all sense of propriety! You've brought nothing but scandal and dishonor to the family since you arrived. Take the money—or don't take it if you're too proud and stubborn to admit you need it—but *leave before you cause any more damage.*"

She turned on her stacked heels and flounced across the unmowed lawn to her car.

Anna leaned against the doorframe, her heart pounding. For a few painful seconds Isabela's words rang with a degree of convincing truth. But as the sun sank behind the rows of fruit trees, Isabela's breathless exhortations and any pretense of sense behind them dissipated into the orange-scented evening.

The idea of Naldo losing all sense of propriety almost made her chuckle. He must have defended Anna's presence to his sister. Told her the cook's daughter was staying put.

A shimmer of pride in Naldo warmed her, along with the tropical evening breeze. Maybe things would work out for the best in ways she couldn't even begin to imagine.

She certainly couldn't predict the future, but one way or another, she was home right now. With that reassuring thought she ate her dinner, went to bed, and drifted into a heavy sleep.

The digital clock read 1:23 a.m. when she woke up. A tickle in her throat alerted her to the smell of smoke in the air.

Smoke? This house didn't even have a fireplace.

She snapped on the light. Everything looked normal. The hum of the air conditioner drowned out other sounds as she strained to hear something. But something was wrong.

Adrenaline sneaked through her as she climbed out of bed, the acrid smell stinging her nostrils. On instinct she pulled a T-shirt and shorts over her flimsy pajamas and slipped her feet into sneakers.

The bare bulb in the hallway made her blink. She still smelled smoke, not any stronger though. Not thick even.

Nerves crackling, she tiptoed downstairs.

Then she saw it.

An orange fireball of flame framed by the kitchen window. It took a moment to figure out that it was her van, totally engulfed, flames leaping several feet into the air and sending a shower of sparks into the black night.

She grabbed the phone and dialed 911, her breath coming in hard gasps. She struggled to stay calm as she described the emergency, but as soon as she hung up the phone she let out a shriek of terror as she ran for the garden hose.

Where was it? She could barely remember the location of the outdoor faucet in the smoke-thickened darkness. The roar of the fire was deafening. Her heart flew to her throat as she realized that if the van exploded the house would catch fire. The burning vehicle was parked only a few yards away, right on the front lawn.

Lucky thing she hadn't been able to afford to refill the tank, she thought grimly, as she struggled with the tangled garden hose and the corroded brass knob in the writhing orange light of the fire. It took a full minute to coax out a stream of water, and that pathetic trickle looked to be no match for the seething, crackling mass of light and sound.

She half gasped, half screamed as she noticed the first trail of fire streaking into the grass. Then another, and another. Flying sparks and flames from the van leapt into the dry, long grass now parched by the nearby inferno.

She turned the hose on the stray embers and they extinguished easily, but as soon as she put one out, three more sprang up, leaping and creeping closer and closer to the cottage.

"Hey!" A shout made her jump. Naldo ran toward her, his face tightened against the heat and light of the flames. "Are you okay? Are you hurt?"

"I'm fine. I just smelled smoke."

"Give me that." He grabbed the hose and started to lay a line of water around the side of the van nearest to the house. But at that moment the windshield exploded.

Naldo hurled himself at her, crushing her hard against the ground, knocking the breath from her lungs. Her knees and elbow stung. "Stay down. The gas tank might blow."

"It's empty," she gasped, under the weight of him. "But there's other stuff in there. All my mom's things."

Her heart stuttered as she thought of all the precious things she'd packed, immolated by the cruel flames.

Naldo scrambled to his feet and pulled her roughly to hers. "I called the fire department, but they're fifteen minutes away. Ricky's getting water from the irrigation house; he should be here any minute. What happened?"

Anna stamped out a spark in the grass, then another, as Naldo poured more water on the scorched grass.

"I don't know. I woke up and smelled smoke." The heat of the fire was becoming unbearable, like fierce midday sun on unprotected skin. "The van was already engulfed."

She stamped and stamped at a stubborn patch of smoldering grass, only to notice too late that a thick ember had leapt from the van onto the grass in front of the steps. In an instant the ancient wood steps ignited, flames licking along the paint and into the dry wood.

Naldo ran forward and poured water on the flames, but the thin stream from the hose was no match for the burst of flame that ran up the wood trim and ignited the small decorative cornice above the door with a loud whoosh.

Anna stamped at the grass, losing ground against the hail of sparks and streams of fire spreading across the lawn in all directions.

The front window of the house exploded, hurling glass at them, and she screamed as she threw up her arms to cover her eyes. Fine particles scratched her skin.

"Are you injured?" Concern contorted Naldo's features.

"Oh, my God. The flames are inside." Through the black hole of the broken window she could see flames roaring up the old flowered curtains.

"Ricky! Drive it right up here." Naldo gestured furiously as a tractor came into view, pulling a big plastic water tank on wheels. Other workers came pelting into view through the thick black smoke, carrying buckets and shovels.

"It's spreading across the road, toward the groves," Ricky shouted through the din of the fire.

"Make a firebreak. Don't let it get into the groves," Naldo shouted back. He seized Anna's arm and pulled her close, his voice right in her ear. "It's probably too late for the cottage. They have to protect the groves. You and I, we'll do what we can."

"Oh, God." An upper-story window blew out and flames shot through the vent of the air conditioner. Naldo tugged her away from the rain of glass and sparks, around to the still dark rear of the house.

Her hands shook. "The cookbook. It's upstairs. I took it up there to read. And the jewels, they're in the attic."

"There's nothing we can do about them."

"I have to save them. I can go up through the back door." She stared at the black rectangle of glass, pulse pounding in her head as adrenaline flooded her limbs. No flames had reached this side of the house yet. There was still a chance.

"No." Naldo seized her arm roughly. "It could go up at any moment." He had already turned the hose onto the dry grass behind the house. Embers were flying through the air thicker and faster as the fire grew. Unmowed and scraggly, the grass pricked her ankles as she hopped from one foot to another, or beat the grass with her bare hands.

"I should have let Ricky mow it," she said quietly, biting back harsh tears rising in her throat.

"Yes." Naldo focused on creating a strip of wet grass about ten yards away from the house, between the fire and the small grove of Summer's Shadow trees his father had planted behind it.

Then he grabbed a shovel from the small tool shed and started to dig a trench behind the area. In no time he'd dug a wide, shallow firebreak across the lawn. Then he started on another. She soaked the grass as far as the hose would reach.

She looked up with a start as the high-pitched wail of the first fire engine pierced the roar of the flames and the roar of panic in her brain. "The fire department is here!"

But already the upper windows now glowed orange with flame.

A window under the roof blew out with little more than a *whoosh* and orange flames licked the gutter.

Unshed tears tightened her throat as panic pounded through her. It was all going up in the merciless rush of flames. The house, the jewels, the cookbook—everything that tied her to Naldo's world.

Ten

A fireman ran around the house. He ripped off his oxygen mask and shouted, "You've got to get out of here. These old houses can blow apart in seconds."

Anna still couldn't process what was happening. Flames now danced along the ridgeline of the roof.

"Come on." Naldo tugged at her arm. "The walls are probably lined with newspaper, it's all over."

"I can't! I can't leave it. All my mother's things!"

"Anna." Naldo put his arm around her. "We've done all we can. Come away before falling debris can hurt you." For a moment the warmth of his strong arm soothed the terror leaping inside her like the bright flames piercing the night.

"Naldo!" A hoarse shout accompanied the appearance of a soot-stained man Anna hadn't seen before. "It's in the old orchard—the branches are dry. It's spreading fast."

Naldo cursed under his breath and tugged her with him as he ran forward. "Anna, you have to go back to the house. Take my car, the keys are in the ignition."

"I can't. I want to help."

"No."

"Please!" How could she go sit in the house when he and the estate were in danger?

Naldo put his hands on her shoulders, his strong fingers gripping her with gentle force. "Everything will be okay." His eyes flashed in the darkness. "But right now you're just one more thing to worry about. Go to the house and tell Pilar I asked her to give you a room."

She hesitated and glanced over her shoulder. The horrifying sight of flames blazing in the wide canopy of a mature orange tree made her throat close tighter than all the smoke billowing in the air.

"Go." Naldo's command wasn't issued politely.

"Okay. Take care of yourself, Naldo."

He looked at her fiercely for a second, pressed a hot, melting kiss to her lips, then turned and jogged across the already burnt grass to where the blaze was spreading through the groves.

Smoke stung her eyes, making it hard to see as she picked her way over the hoses trailing from the well and the pump trucks, past the shouting strangers and flashing lights.

Naldo's car was parked off the road, out in the darkness. She managed to start the unfamiliar ignition with shaking fingers and pull onto the access road. She drove about a hundred yards before the flashing lights of more fire engines made her pull off again to let them pass.

"What have I done?" The sound of her own wail, in the dull artificial silence of the tightly sealed car, scared her almost as much as the fiery disaster spreading behind her.

The house was ablaze with lights and panicked staff members when she pulled up in the circular driveway.

"You're hurt!" Pilar's panicked reaction startled her. She glanced down, half-expecting to see raw, puckered flesh or oozing blood. The sight of her skin and clothes—soot-smudged but undamaged—brought a stinging wave of relief.

"I'm okay, it's just smoke. Are there more engines coming? The fire is spreading."

"Oh, my God." Pilar crossed herself. "They're trying to find trucks around the county. It's been so dry and windy. There are other fires—" She gripped hold of Anna's forearms. "Has anyone been hurt?"

"No one was injured when I left, but they had an ambulance standing by." She'd seen it, with the doors open and a gurney already set up in anticipation of casualties.

Please don't let Naldo get hurt.

"You!" A shout from the top of the stairway made her look up. Isabela stood on the landing, her long black hair streaming over her shoulders. "This is all your fault! I warned you. I knew that you staying here would bring disaster." She clutched a big lavender handkerchief to her face. "Is my brother safe?"

"Yes." Anna's voice came out very quiet and subdued. "He stayed to fight the fire in the groves."

"The groves are burning?" Isabela stared at her, black eyes boring a hole right through her.

She nodded.

"I told you to leave. I told you!" With a dramatic sob, Isabela turned in a swirl of chiffon and marched off down the hall. Anna heard a door slam.

"She's highly strung." Pilar placed a soothing hand on Anna's arm. "She doesn't mean what she's saying.

She's just worried about her brother. He's the only family she has left."

Anna sucked in a shaky breath. *Maybe Isabela was right, and it was her fault that the estate was under siege.*

"Why don't you go take a shower. I'll make up a spare room for you."

"Okay." Anna let Pilar lead her upstairs into the brightly lit hallway. She showed her into a vast bedroom decorated with a sunny floral motif, and ushered her into the big, adjoining bathroom.

Anna avoided the sight of her shocked and dirty face in the bathroom mirror. She peeled off her clothes and climbed under the hot stream of water.

The thought of Naldo out in the heat and smoke and flames made her heart clench with terror.

I do love him. I know I do.

By the time she'd emerged from the steaming water, someone had whisked away her dirty clothes and a simple cotton nightgown—probably one of Pilar's—was laid on the bed.

Dressed, she took a deep breath as she pulled up the window sash. The room faced away from the fire, but she could still smell smoke in the air and hear distant shouts.

The reality of the situation sucked the wind from her lungs.

Everything was gone. Not just her mother's sentimental treasures—the old alarm clock, the porcelain figures, the silly seashells—but the cookbook, the cottage.

The jewels.

Naldo's family treasures would be nothing but dust and ashes by now. Why had pigheaded stubbornness made her keep them back at the cottage when they would have been so much more secure here in a safe at the house?

She'd proved her point all right: the cottage and the land and the jewels were all *hers*. Her very own pile of smoking rubble.

And probably all uninsured, in the De Leon tradition.

Her fingers turned cold despite the hot smoky breeze pouring through the windows. She pulled down the sash.

A knock on the door made her jump. "Come in."

She turned and saw a strange man in uniform. "Ms. Marcus?"

"Yes."

"Investigator Davis. I'd like to ask you a few questions about how the fire got started."

"Oh." A rush of cool fear washed through her. Did they think she'd started it? "I don't know how it began. I woke up and smelled smoke."

"May I come in?" He took a step into the room even as he asked the question.

"Um, sure." She ushered him to a sofa with a cheerful leaf pattern.

He was young, with bright blue eyes and ruddy razor-burned cheeks. "I understand you and Mr. De Leon were having some kind of disagreement over the cottage and the land?"

"No, not at all. He wanted to buy it from me and I intended to sell it."

"But you hadn't sold it."

"No, not yet, but I… Am I suspected of something?"

"We're investigating the cause of the fire. There's a possibility that accelerants were used. Traces of gasoline were found on the lawn near the cottage."

A single name instantly tumbled into Anna's mind.

Isabela.

Naldo's sister obviously hated her and wanted her gone.

She'd planted the article in the paper, wanting to stir up trouble. She might be just crazy enough to start a fire in order to get rid of her.

She drew in a breath to steady herself. "I think I know who might have started it."

Anna hovered behind the closed door of her room as all hell broke loose.

Predictably, Isabela didn't take well to being questioned by an officious young policeman. Finally, she insulted Officer Davis in French and slapped him hard across the cheek, which led to her being taken to the station.

The way she screamed and cried in protest as they dragged her away made Anna even more sure that she was guilty.

Once Isabela was gone, a painful silence fell over the house. Anna slipped out of the bedroom to see if she could get any news on the fire and on Naldo.

She found Pilar weeping at the large granite island in the kitchen with Tom, one of the other staff members, consoling her.

"Poor Miss Isabela. Naldo will be so upset when he finds out. First the fire, and now this!" She let out a wail.

Anna froze in the kitchen doorway. "Did they take her for questioning?"

"They arrested her! She assaulted an officer." Pilar sobbed into a paper towel. "She has a terrible temper, she's so proud, but she'd never do anything like this, never!"

"The fire, is there any news?"

"Yes. Thank goodness, they have it under control. Naldo just called. They're soaking down the ground and breaking the cottage apart to make sure there are no burning embers." She looked up at Anna with teary eyes. "I'm sorry about your mother's cottage."

"Me, too." But relief roared through her that Naldo was alive and that the fire was over. All she wanted was to feel his strong arms around her again, to hear him reassure her once more that everything would be okay.

"Naldo's back!" A young employee burst through the door with the news that made Anna jump to her feet. She ran out into the hallway.

"Naldo!"

He was filthy from head to toe but alive and unharmed. "They took Isabela." Disbelief echoed in his voice. He strode up to Anna and seized her arm. His eyes shone with a look she'd never seen there before. "Why?"

"They think she may have started the fire."

He shook his head and incredulity creased his smudged features. "It's ridiculous." He let go of her arm. "I'm going to the station."

Adrenaline zipped through her at the thought of losing him again already. "But Naldo, think about it. She might have started the fire to get rid of me. She came to me last night and told me that by staying I'd only bring disaster—"

His black stare withered the rest of the words on her tongue. "You think my own sister would start a fire on the estate? She's a difficult woman, I won't deny it, but she's family and I know her like I know myself. She would *never* do something like this." He'd already turned and strode toward the door.

"If she's innocent, she'll be fine. Please don't go—" The front door slammed behind him as he swept out into the night.

Of course Isabela started the fire. Naturally, that was hard for Naldo to accept, but once he thought about it, he'd see the sense in it.

Unease prickled along her arms to her fingers and made her shiver in her borrowed robe.

"You accused Miss Isabela?" Pilar's voice, right behind her, made her jump.

"I… She came to me yesterday evening, threatened me." She turned to face her.

Pilar looked stunned. One of the most respected employees on the estate, she had reputedly come from Spain with Naldo's mother some forty years earlier. No doubt her loyalty to the family prevented her from seeing what Isabela was capable of.

The older woman stared at her, lips parted.

Tom stepped between them and placed his hand on Anna's arm. "Everyone's safe from the fire. Why don't you get some sleep?"

She nodded, anxious to get away from the housekeeper's accusing eyes. No way could she sleep, but maybe she could just lie down and catch her breath until Naldo got back.

As a thick, warm finger of sun crept across the bed and pointed directly at her face, Anna opened her eyes.

She sat up with a jolt, heart pounding.

I fell asleep?

How had she managed to drift off amidst all the drama? She scrambled out of bed and padded across the cool, polished wood to the wide, arched window. By the height of the sun it must be at least nine o'clock.

She turned and saw her clothes, freshly laundered and laid out on the chaise at the end of the bed. Next to them was that morning's issue of the *Sunshine Post*.

Fire at De Leon Estate screamed the headline. Her heart in her throat, Anna scanned the byline. Different reporter, thank goodness.

Fire ripped through an old estate cottage, sparking a brushfire that destroyed several acres of orange groves late last night. The Round Lake fire department responded along with engines from several nearby companies, and the blaze was reported to be under control at the time of going to press.

Known as Paradiso, the De Leon estate boasts more than four hundred years of existence, so this is not the first setback they've weathered, but could it be the last?

Elder daughter Isabela De Leon was questioned by police last night amid rumors that she's bitter about her brother inheriting the entire estate. Is she suspected of setting the blaze?

Gossip that the fire in the dilapidated worker's cottage could be a scam to collect insurance on the old structure were soon quashed by the disturbing news that the De Leons have always scorned insurance, like the British Royal family whose Windsor Castle was uninsured when it burned to the tune of 90 million dollars in 1992.

Will Round Lake's "royal family" survive this latest blow in the wake of patriarch Robert De Leon's death? Or will the younger family members—beset by inheritance squabbles and lacking the experience of their forebears—decide to throw in a four-hundred-year-old towel and sell up? There are plenty of developers who'd like to bite off a piece of the largest privately owned estate in Central Florida.

Anna closed her eyes and leaned against a bedpost. Naldo would go through the roof when he saw this. It amounted to a personal insult to him and his ability to run the family and the estate.

Her name wasn't mentioned, which probably only meant they hadn't figured out the cottage that burned was the one she and Naldo were wrangling over. But when they did…

Her heart thumped so hard she had to gasp for air. Where was Naldo? She needed to see him, to see his face, to reassure herself—

Of what? That he didn't curse her and the ground she walked on?

Someone had obviously put a lot of effort into cleaning her clothes and sneakers, which was good as they were the only clothes she had in the world right now. The grim thought drove home the ugly desperation of her predicament.

No van. No cottage. No gems. No money.

Somehow it was all too awful to seem real, and wouldn't really sink in. She kept trying to reassure herself that things would "be okay," as Naldo had predicted.

Would they?

As she ran her fingers through her uncombed hair and wished she had a scrap of makeup to paint a brave face on, a commotion from downstairs made her ears prick up.

She turned the brass doorknob and stepped out into the second-floor hallway. Silhouetted below in the sunlit doorway stood Naldo, his arm wrapped tightly around a weeping and obviously hysterical Isabela.

Anna shrank back into her room for a second.

"Fetch some iced tea," Naldo barked. "Get some food for her. Those beasts had her up all night."

He'd found the time to shower and change. He looked crisp and elegant in a dark suit.

His face, however, looked blacker than ever. Not from soot, but from dark, seething anger. Anna's empty stomach started to knot.

Isabela looked shockingly tragic, leaning in her tall brother's arms, her long black hair hanging wild to her waist and her eyes ringed with smudged mascara. Naldo spoke some soft words to her that Anna didn't catch, then began to help her across the wide, marble-floored foyer toward the living room.

Suddenly he glanced up.

His gaze seized Anna's and held her fast like a rat in a trap. Her mouth fell open, but words didn't come out.

"How could you do this?" His voice rang coldly through the huge foyer. "How could you accuse *my sister* of this terrible crime?" Isabela pressed her head to his shoulder, and he stroked her disordered hair.

"As I suspected, it was *your van* that started the fire. That deathtrap on wheels had an electrical malfunction and *that* is what started the blaze. The accelerant on the grass occurs only in places where you'd parked your van and carelessly allowed its *leaking fuel tank* to spill gasoline onto the grass where it could feed the flames."

"Oh." She bit her lip.

Hard.

Until it hurt.

He'd offered to call his mechanic. She knew the van leaked a bit, but never thought much of it. Didn't all old cars leak?

"The cottage," she stammered. "Did anything survive?"

"Nothing." Naldo held her gaze for one more searing moment, then turned and walked toward the living room, his arm around his sister.

Throughout this exchange Isabela was uncharacteristically silent. In fact she seemed somehow…pathetic.

Even Anna couldn't imagine this shaking, weeping woman being the type to slosh gasoline around a house and set a match to it.

Isabela was wealthy and had a life in Europe. Sure, she wanted Anna gone, but enough to jeopardize her freedom?

Hardly.

And would someone so neurotically concerned about her reputation risk making the papers as a jealous arsonist?

No way.

The grave error of her accusation began to sink in, turning her fingers and toes to ice. She slid back into the bedroom and closed the door.

Family and the estate were everything to Naldo. She'd injured both in ways that could never be put right.

In that instant she knew nothing would ever be "okay" again.

Eleven

Naldo didn't come to her room. Eventually she crept downstairs, heart in her mouth. She heard voices on the other side of the living room door, which was uncharacteristically closed. Should she go in and apologize?

I'm sorry about my pigheaded refusal to maintain my van or admit that I couldn't afford it. I'm sorry I wouldn't let your gardener cut the grass. I'm sorry I kept the gems in the cottage. I'm sorry I didn't just take your money and go when I had the chance....

She clenched her hands so tight that her nails dug into the skin of her palms.

I'm sorry I fell in love with you and didn't want to leave.

It was all her fault. And now all her hopeful fantasies of living here in Paradiso had come to smoldering ruin.

She'd accused his sister of arson. Yes, Isabela was an

opera diva to the core, but an arsonist and potential murderer?

Anna blew out a hard breath. She needed to apologize to Isabela.

She straightened her shoulders, lifted her chin and marched to the living room door.

Her hand shook as she reached for the ornate brass knob and turned it. The voices hushed as she pulled open the heavy door. Everyone turned to stare.

Isabela lay on the sofa, her head resting on Pilar's lap while Pilar braided her long hair.

An older man she recognized as a lawyer from the will reading sat in a wingback chair while Tom refilled his glass with iced tea from a large jug.

No sign of Naldo.

As soon as Isabela saw her she sat up, tugging her braid from Pilar's fingers. "You? What are you still doing here? You gold-digging whore, get out!"

Anna's apology evaporated into a mist of indignation. "I'm not a gold digger. I've never wanted anything but what's rightfully mine."

"Dennis, how much exactly did you say the contract gave her?"

The lawyer placed his hand on a sheaf of papers in his lap. "Four million dollars."

"Four million dollars." Isabela's eyes narrowed. In pants and a plain shirt, and without her usual glossy makeup, she looked younger and more ordinary, and somehow far more dangerous. "My brother offered you four million dollars, but that wasn't enough for you, was it?"

"I was planning to accept the money."

"Oh? You were *planning* to take it? And there was my poor brother thinking you were too noble or some such rubbish. I knew better all along. Give me the contract, Dennis."

She leaned forward and snatched it from his hand. "Four million dollars." She looked up at Anna. "For the jewels, which are now *destroyed*."

Anna bit the inside of her mouth. Isabela traced a line in the contract with a nail. "For the *cottage*, which is a heap of charred *rubble*." Her icy stare made Anna's shoulders tighten. "For some cookbook that is now a pile of cinders, and for the *land*."

Isabela rose to her feet, which were uncharacteristically bare. She walked around the coffee table and pointed an accusatory finger at Anna. "That's my brother's land, and you know it. Do you still mean to try to extort money from him after all the destruction you've caused? Five acres of orange groves *burned*. Do you know how much that hurts Naldo? He loves those trees, like, like—"

"Like family." Anna heard her own voice as if it was someone else's. The room and everyone in it felt strangely disconnected from her, as if she'd already left it. "May I have the contract?"

"You can't sign it now." Isabela's eyes narrowed. "You have nothing to bargain with."

"Here's another copy." Dennis fished one out of a leather case on the floor beside his chair. "I'm sure Mr. De Leon would like to resolve the matter of the land if you could see your way to—"

"Do you have a pen?" Anna interrupted him, her voice shaking.

"Of course." He produced a tortoiseshell ballpoint pen from an inner pocket of his suit jacket.

She flipped through the contract to the page where the

amount of money was printed. $4,000,000. It didn't look real, even as she crossed out the full amount with the ball-point pen and wrote in the number one. "The land is his," she croaked.

She cleared her throat. "Does anyone have a dollar to pay me for it? I want it to be legal and I know the exchange of money is an important part of—"

"Here." Dennis whipped a dollar out of a billfold inside his jacket.

Anna took the single dollar bill and signed her name on the final page. "It's done." She handed it to the lawyer.

Isabela's mouth sat in a grim line, but satisfaction shone in her eyes.

"Where's Naldo?" It took the rest of Anna's courage to ask the question.

"He's at the courthouse." Isabela spoke calmly. "Trying to persuade them to drop the charges against me. I'm accused of assaulting an officer and resisting arrest." She stared at Anna for a withering second. "Of course we both know why I resisted arrest, don't we? *Because I was being falsely accused of a crime I did not commit.*" She crossed her arms over her ample chest. "Please, don't wait for Naldo. He does *not* wish to see you."

Anna blinked. Her usual fire seemed to have flickered out and there was nothing left but smoke and ash. Like the smoke and ash that remained of her mother's precious things and all her hopes and dreams.

Isabela strode past her and pulled open the door to the room. She held it, and gestured for Anna to leave.

She left.

No one was in the foyer as she made her exit, clutch-ing one worn dollar bill. A burned smell hung in the air as she made her way down the front steps.

You came here with nothing, and you're leaving with nothing.

And that's okay.

She was uninjured, which was a huge blessing under the circumstances. She was young and strong and smart and hard-working.

She owed the local motel two hundred and thirty dollars.

The motel owners seemed like a nice couple. Perhaps they'd let her work off her bill? It was worth a try.

Pay off her bill and get out of town. She'd always been a planner, but right now that was as far as her grand schemes extended.

She set out through the groves in the direction of the motel, which sat outside Round Lake on an empty stretch of highway. She knew the land like she knew her own body, and the cross-country route would be quicker. She could avoid the sight of the burned cottage she didn't want to lay eyes on, and this route had the advantage of keeping her off the long driveway so she wouldn't run into Naldo on his way back from the courthouse.

At the thought of him, her stomach clenched and her throat tightened. She didn't want to see the disgusted look he'd have on his face when he thought of her.

He'd offered her so much. And she'd turned her nose up at it and caused irreparable damage to the estate and to his sister's reputation. Would he ever forgive her for all the harm she'd caused?

How could he? The family jewels he'd wanted so badly were gone forever. The cookbook his father had lovingly illustrated was destroyed, along with all traces of her mother and the love they'd quietly shared for so many years.

A breeze rustled the shiny leaves around her as she

marched through the sandy soil down a long, fragrant row of orange-laden trees. The sun shone bright overhead in a sharp blue sky, already burning her uncovered skin.

Paradiso was not to be her home.

For the first time in her life she felt truly alone. She'd wanted it all and held out for everything.

She cringed as she thought how after the latest altercation over the cookbook Naldo must think she'd wanted a stake in the estate. What she'd really wanted was a stake in his heart.

Her uncompromising attitude and stiff-necked pride had left her with nothing, and no one. Her mother may not have been called Mrs. De Leon, but at least she had love and affection and a place to call home.

Her journey took her into a grove of early-bearing trees in full fragrant flower, then into a grove where oranges hung heavy on the branches, ready to be plucked and eaten.

She'd had no breakfast and her stomach growled with increasing ferocity as her legs ached from her long walk. The lush, round oranges called to her, with their delicious rich scent and deep color. But she'd rather starve than take yet one more thing from Naldo. She didn't deserve it.

It was past noon, the harsh sun burning overhead like a movie spotlight, by the time she approached the county road. She could just make out the rumble of a big transport truck, maybe taking oranges for processing. The soles of her feet pricked and tickled inside her hot sneakers as her footsteps slowed. Once she left the estate, this was it.

Goodbye.

Her footsteps slowed in the heat and the dry dust in the air. The sand beneath her feet seemed heavy, pulling her back. The sun hurt her head and an agonizing sense of loss hurt her heart.

Her pulse started to pound in her head with irregular beats that made her press her fingers to her temples. Her own heart sounded almost like the muffled thuds of a horse's hooves.

Then again, it sounded like a real horse's hooves. Was there a horse nearby? The ghost of a De Leon ancestor so enraged by her presence on his sacred turf that he'd come to scare her off?

A breathy snort in the next row of trees told her a real beast was very close. She stopped walking and stood still, terror streaking along her nerves.

It couldn't really be a ghost. The foreman come to investigate a report of trespassing?

The hoofbeats moved farther away, and she pressed her hand to her pounding heart. Almost at the road. The roar of a tanker passing at high speed didn't sound any less appealing than the mysterious horseman, but at least it was familiar.

Suddenly a huge black horse crashed through the trees right in front of her. At the sight of her it whinnied and reared high in the air, hooves flailing. She shrieked and the rider turned the horse hard in a circle and brought it to a panting halt.

Naldo.

He jumped down, holding the reins.

Her blood pounded in her brain as she stood there wordless, rooted in the sandy soil. Naldo's face wore a stony expression. His hair wet with perspiration and tossed by the wind, his white dress shirt flung open at the collar, he looked wild—and dangerous.

"Where are you going?" His deep voice thundered with accusation.

She straightened her shoulders. "I'm leaving. You won't

see me again." She swallowed. "I apologize for all the harm I caused. It wasn't intended."

Naldo stared at her for one intense second then blew out an exasperated blast of air. "You think you can just *leave?*"

She blinked rapidly. "I deeded you the land. I know the land is all that's left now. I'm sorry." Her legs felt weak. How could she think that one lousy acre of land would make up for the loss of the gems, the cottage, the orchards...

"The land?" His mouth curved into a snarl of disgust. "You really are crazy."

The horse jerked at the reins and Naldo soothed it with a word, then turned back to her, eyes blazing. "You think it's all just about the money?"

The force of his stare made her shiver. "I know you must think I've behaved badly."

"Yes." He nodded. A strange spark appeared in his eyes. "You're damn right. For someone so smart, you act very dumb sometimes."

Anger tightened her muscles as her heart started to break right in two. Naldo *hated* her. "Don't insult me. I know I owe you. I'll pay you back. I made a mistake. Anyone can make a mistake."

"*A mistake?* Only one? Let's see...refusing to maintain your van, refusing to mow the grass, insisting on keeping the gems, refusing to take the very large amount of money I offered you, accusing my sister of arson—"

"Are you going to sue me?" She held her chin high, proud of the way she kept her voice steady.

'I probably should." He petted the neck of his restless horse again. His eyes glinted with a strange look she'd never seen before. "But I wouldn't dare." He let out a chuckle. "You're far too dangerous as an opponent. Lord knows, next time I go up against you I might lose my shirt."

He looked like he was in danger of losing his shirt anyway, with the buttons undone in front to reveal a broad strip of tan muscle. A stray rush of heat made her cringe.

"You love this place, don't you?" Naldo's question, spoken softly, took her by surprise.

"Yes," she whispered, without thinking.

"That's why you couldn't leave. Why you wouldn't take the money." His eyes narrowed as his head tilted very slightly.

Tears rose in her throat, and she gulped them away. She nodded, afraid to speak and have her words come out pathetically teary.

"You truly are crazy, Anna." He shook his head. His majestic brow furrowed. "I offered you four million dollars. Do you have any idea what most people would do for four million dollars?"

She shook her head, still afraid to speak.

"And you wouldn't take it. It just wasn't quite enough for you." He looked at her steadily, black eyes boring into her.

"I know you think I'm greedy," she protested, as the silence threatened to steal her last breath.

"I know you're greedy," he responded. He took a step forward. "So am I. We're alike, you and I." He stared at her with force. "We both want it all and can't settle for anything less. It's not in us."

Her heart thumped painfully as he took another step toward her and dropped his horse's reins. The intense look in his eyes stole her breath. Did he mean to destroy her? To exact revenge in the way that only a man with the wealth, power and influence of a De Leon could?

He could make sure she never worked again. That she never had a penny to eat with. That anything she might achieve could be seized in reparation for the terrible mistake of crossing Naldo De Leon.

The fire in her flickered back to life. "I know you must hate me. And why not? I'm hard and tough and unfeminine. I'm ambitious and aggressive and competitive and all those things that women aren't supposed to be." She lifted her chin. "I'm a bitch. There I've said it. It's nothing I didn't already hear a hundred times from my ex-husband." She paused and sucked in a shaky breath. "You can hate me all you want, and trust me, you won't hate me as much as I hate myself right now, but don't poison your life or mine by seeking revenge on me."

She searched his face for his reaction. His brows had lowered and his eyes narrowed to dark slits. A storm cloud of angry emotion covered his features.

"Damn it, Anna—" His eyes flashed.

She had no idea what he was about to say next, because he grabbed her around the waist and arrested her lips with a brutal kiss.

Heat surged through her, roaring along her limbs, firing her heart and lungs. As Naldo's tongue pushed into her mouth, she pressed herself against him, desperate to hold tight to his hard body. Thoughts deserted her in a wash of stinging relief at being in Naldo's arms again.

Nothing mattered but being here, right now, in Naldo's angry, hungry embrace. His long fingers shoved into her hair, gripping her skull, pressing her face to his with feverish intensity.

She heard his groan, low and coarse, and felt the strength of his feeling in the way he held her like he couldn't ever let go. She clung to him even tighter.

"I love you, Naldo."

She didn't care if he knew. If he'd mock her for it. All the mistakes she'd made stemmed from that simple fact.

"I know." He pulled back a few inches, holding her face

in his hands, his eyes and lips inches from hers. His hot breath tickled her skin. "I love you too, Anna."

Her heart tightened into a fist as feelings too powerful to name or comprehend surged through her.

Naldo pushed a strand of hair roughly but tenderly off her face. Passion burned in his eyes. "I love the way you fight for what you want, that you can't settle for less."

He lowered his lips to hers and kissed them. His touch was gentle, but the force of his emotion stung her. He pulled back again, his breath and hers coming in unsteady gasps.

His broad thumb caressed her cheek. "I know you love the estate. I've seen it in your eyes, and in the way you couldn't sell out and give up your home here, even for more money than most people ever dream of." His black eyes shone. "Stay here with me, Anna."

Every nerve in her screamed the word *yes*, but it didn't emerge from her mouth. Her brain was more cautious. "I don't want to be your girlfriend, Naldo. Here at your discretion, until you tire of me."

"Of course you don't. That's why I love you. All-or-nothing Anna." Humor flashed in his eyes, then faded. "When they told me you'd gone—" He shook his head and blew out a breath. "I need you, Anna. I need you here, with me."

Still holding her hand he lowered himself heavily down onto one black-suit-pant-covered knee in the sandy soil.

Anna's pulse pounded at her temple as her hopes soared far beyond any safe level.

He took her hand, which was shaking like an orange blossom. "Anna." His face was solemn. "I love you and I promise to care for you and cherish you always if you will do me the honor of becoming my wife."

His words swam in her brain and she wasn't sure she'd

understood them right. He held her gaze with frightening intensity. "Will you marry me?"

"Yes." The word flew from her mouth, and in an instant Naldo was on his feet, enveloping her in his strong embrace.

Tears streamed down her cheeks and she wasn't even embarrassed.

Naldo's big hands roamed over her back, chafing her skin through her T-shirt, sending shivers of happiness through her. "You belong here, just like I do."

His strong arms wrapped around her and held her tight. She pressed her cheek to the hard muscle of his chest, tears wetting his shirt and skin. "I do. This is the only place I've ever felt at home, and you're the only man I've ever truly loved." Her voice emerged as a whisper.

Naldo threaded his fingers into her hair. "Sometimes you have to lose something to know how much you need it." His voice resonated with emotion. "I don't ever want to lose you again, Anna."

She shuddered at the realization of how close she'd come to losing Naldo along with everything else. "I'm so sorry about the trees and the jewels and the cottage. If only I'd…"

"Shh." Naldo put his finger on her lips. "They're just things." He kissed her wet lashes and drew in a ragged breath. "They have no value compared to a lifetime together." He buried his face in her neck, his breath hot on her skin, and she hugged him with all her might. Her heart swelled painfully and she wondered if it could just burst from too much joy.

"I'm glad to be home." She breathed the words into his warm, fragrant skin. Birds chirped in the trees and the horse nickered peacefully nearby as Naldo held her steady in his powerful embrace.

The warm sun and gentle breeze kissed their skin, and Anna could almost feel herself sending down roots into the rich, fertile soil, drawing strength to grow a vigorous new branch on the four-hundred-year-old family tree planted here.

Epilogue

"It's like a miracle." Anna sat on a blanket next to Naldo, as sun filtered through leafy branches in the Summer's Shadow orchard. Less than six months had passed since the fire and the trees were ablaze with lush green foliage.

"It's nature. I guess it is a miracle." Naldo rubbed a broad hand over the rough bark of the trunk. "You can see how the burned bark has healed over and trees have put out new shoots where the dead branches were cut away." He reached up and took a shiny new leaf between finger and thumb. "The life force of the tree is strong. It's in their nature to heal and recover."

"Just like it's in ours." She took his hand and squeezed it. "Your dad would be so proud of what you've done in the orchards, and how you've brought the family back together."

"Me? You can take the credit for making Isabela happy.

I can't believe you talked me into buying her that big vineyard in the Loire Valley."

"She deserves it after what I put her through." She still cringed inwardly when she remembered that night.

"Stop feeling guilty." Naldo stroked her cheek with his knuckle. "That whole experience knocked down a lot of the walls between us. We've been getting along much better since then."

"True. She had a blast at the wedding. No wonder the paparazzi love her, she knows how to party. I can't believe all those photographers flew here from Europe."

"It was 'the wedding of the decade.'" Naldo winked.

"Geez. We only had a thousand guests! I don't know what the big deal is. You ask a few buddies over and suddenly you're big news. At least we don't have to worry about not having enough wedding pictures." She pretended to take a picture of Naldo. "Seriously, though, I'm glad I made up with Isabela. I'm looking forward to visiting her. She even suggested I should come up with some products to make with the grapes from her estate. I guess she's not horrified by my culinary roots anymore."

"Yeah, not since you turned out to be a genius in the kitchen yourself. Speaking of which, don't you have a new product to test on me?"

"I might." She reached into the old picnic basket and pulled out a small mason jar with a mischievous smile on her face. She couldn't help a rush of pride that she'd inherited her mom's talent for cooking.

Naldo lay back, hands behind his head, as she unscrewed it, dipped a finger into the jar and brought it out glistening with amber liquid. "Try it."

Naldo obediently sucked the tip of her finger, dark eyes fixed on hers. "Mmm-hmm. Orange and ginger."

He licked his lips. "Can I spread it all over you and lick it off?"

Her skin stirred as she imagined the rasp of his lips and tongue on her aroused flesh. "That would be a very thorough taste-testing."

He lowered his head, a gleam in his eyes. "It's this kind of hard work that's grown our retail sales by two hundred percent in the last year. We owe it to our customers."

"So true. We mustn't neglect our duties."

"Spoken like a true De Leon. But before we eat, I have something for you," he whispered into her hair.

She fought the urge to smile. "Let me guess, another gem?"

"Smart as well as beautiful." Naldo fished a box out of his pants pocket. "Check it out. Narciso's outdone himself with this one."

Anna took the box, a smile creeping across her mouth. Naldo's old family jewels had been found amidst the charred ruins of the cottage. The box had burned to nothing and the dated settings melted into the ash, but the brilliant gems had emerged from the fire unscathed.

Naldo was getting a ridiculous amount of pleasure having them reset by a friend of his from college who'd become a renowned jewelry designer.

"Wow." She lifted out a large brilliant stone glittering at the center of several interwoven strands of gold. "Is this the Star of the Sea? The one from India?"

He nodded, his dimples appearing. "Yes, carried here by my ancestor Pedro Amador De Leon. He fought a maharaja's tiger to win it. May I put in on you?"

"Sure." She couldn't help grinning. "I feel kind of bad for the tiger, but it is amazing. It's huge!"

His fingers tickled the back of her neck as he fastened

the clasp. She sensed his smile beaming down on her from behind. It was sweet how Naldo loved to pamper her with his family treasures, and damn if it didn't feel good to be cherished.

As she turned to face him, he glanced at the gem resting between her collarbones then raised his intense gaze to meet hers.

"Exquisite."

He said the word looking into her eyes, so she wasn't sure if he meant the priceless diamond in its elegant new setting…

Or *her*.

Her answer came when he closed his lips over hers in a greedy kiss.

She kissed him back hard, pushing her fingers into his thick hair and inhaling the intoxicating outdoor scent of his suntanned skin.

When they pulled apart, Naldo whispered into her ear. "I love you, Mrs. De Leon."

She shivered with raw pleasure. Somehow she never got tired of her new name. Not because of the status and power that came with it, but because she shared it with the man she loved.

Four hundred years of growth, change and the resilient force of life hummed in the soil, in the trees and the air. As her lips stung with their kiss, Anna had a sudden, fierce sense of their place in that cycle, as heirs to a legacy of passion—for the land and for each other—that nothing could destroy.

* * * * *

Silhouette® Romantic Suspense
keeps getting hotter!
Turn the page for a sneak preview of
Wendy Rosnau's latest SPY GAMES *title*
SLEEPING WITH DANGER

Available November 2007

Silhouette® Romantic Suspense—
Sparked by Danger, Fueled by Passion!

Melita had been expecting a chaste quick kiss of the generic variety. But this kiss with Sully was the kind that sparked a dying flame to life. The kind of kiss you can't plan for. The kind of kiss memories are built on.

The memory of her murdered lover, Nemo, came to her then and she made a starved little noise in the back of her throat. She raised her arms and threaded her fingers through Sully's hair, pulled him closer. Felt his body settle, then melt into her.

In that instant her hunger for him grew, and his for her. She pressed herself to him with more urgency, and he responded in kind.

Melita came out of her kiss-induced memory of Nemo with a start. "Wait a minute." She pushed Sully away from her. "You bastard!"

She spit two nasty words at him in Greek, then wiped his kiss from her lips.

"I thought you deserved some solid proof that I'm still in one piece." He started for the door. "The clock's ticking, honey. Come on, let's get out of here."

"That's it? You sucker me into kissing you, and that's all you have to say?"

"I'm sorry. How's that?"

He didn't sound sorry in the least. "You're—"

"Getting out of this godforsaken prison cell. Stop whining and let's go."

"Not if I was being shot at sunrise. Go. You deserve whatever you get if you walk out that door."

He turned back. "Freedom is what I'm going to get."

"A second of freedom before the guards in the hall shoot you." She jammed her hands on her hips. "And to think I was worried about you."

"If you're staying behind, it's no skin off my ass."

"Wait! What about our deal?"

"You just said you're not coming. Make up your mind."

"Have you forgotten we need a boat?"

"How could I? You keep harping on it."

"I'm not going without a boat. And those guards out there aren't going to just let you walk out of here. You need me and we need a plan."

"I already have a plan. I'm getting out of here. That's the plan."

"I should have realized that you never intended to take me with you from the very beginning. You're a liar and a coward."

Of everything she had read, there was nothing in Sully Paxton's file that hinted he was a coward, but it was the one word that seemed to register in that one-track mind of his. The look he nailed her with a second later was pure venom.

He came at her so quickly she didn't have time to get out of his way. "You know I'm not a coward."

"Prove it. Give me until dawn. I need one more night to put everything in place before we leave the island."

"You're asking me to stay in this cell one more night... and trust you?"

"Yes."

He snorted. "Yesterday you knew they were planning to harm me, but instead of doing something about it you went to bed and never gave me a second thought. Suppose tonight you do the same. By tomorrow I might damn well be in my grave."

"Okay, I screwed up. I won't do it again." Melita sucked in a ragged breath. "I can't leave this minute. Dawn, Sully. Wait until dawn." When he looked as if he was about to say no, she pleaded, "Please wait for me."

"You're asking a lot. The door's open now. I would be a fool to hang around here and trust that you'll be back."

"What you can trust is that I want off this island as badly as you do, and you're my only hope."

"I must be crazy."

"Is that a yes?"

"Dammit!" He turned his back on her. Swore twice more.

"You won't be sorry."

He turned around. "I already am. How about we seal this new deal?"

He was staring at her lips. Suddenly Melita knew what he expected. "We already sealed it."

"One more. You enjoyed it. Admit it."

"I enjoyed it because I was kissing someone else."

He laughed. "That's a good one."

"It's true. It might have been your lips, but it wasn't you I was kissing."

"If that's your excuse for wanting to kiss me, then—"

"I was kissing Nemo."

"What's a nemo?"

Melita gave Sully a look that clearly told him that he was trespassing on sacred ground. She was about to enforce it with a warning when a voice in the hall jerked them both to attention.

She bolted away from the wall. "Get back in bed. Hurry. I'll be here before dawn."

She didn't reach the door before he snagged her arm, pulled her up against him and planted a kiss on her lips that took her completely by surprise.

When he released her, he said, "If you're confused about who just kissed you, the name's Sully. I'll be here waiting at dawn. Don't be late."

Silhouette®

Romantic
SUSPENSE

**Sparked by Danger,
Fueled by Passion.**

Onyxx agent Sully Paxton's only chance of
survival lies in the hands of his enemy's daughter
Melita Krizova. He doesn't know he's a pawn in the
beautiful island girl's own plan for escape. Can
they survive their ruses and their fiery attraction?

*Look for the next installment in the
Spy Games miniseries,*

*Sleeping with
Danger*
by Wendy Rosnau

Available November 2007 wherever you buy books.

REQUEST YOUR FREE BOOKS!

2 FREE NOVELS PLUS 2 FREE GIFTS!

Passionate, Powerful, Provocative!

SDES07

HARLEQUIN®

Mediterranean NIGHTS™

*Not everything is above board
on Alexandra's Dream!*

*Enjoy plenty of secrets, drama and sensuality
in the latest from Mediterranean Nights.*

Coming in November 2007...

BELOW DECK

by

Dorien Kelly

Determined to protect her young son,
widow Mei Lin Wang keeps him hidden
aboard *Alexandra's Dream* under cover of
her job. But life gets extremely complicated
when the ship's security officer, Gideon Dayan,
is piqued by the mystery surrounding this
beautiful, haunted woman....

HARLEQUIN Romance.

New York Times bestselling author

DIANA PALMER

Handsome, eligible ranch owner Stuart York knew
Ivy Conley was too young for him, so he closed his heart
to her and sent her away—despite the fireworks between
them. Now, years later, Ivy is determined not to be
treated like a little girl anymore…but for some reason,
Stuart is always fighting her battles for her. And safe in
Stuart's arms makes Ivy feel like a woman…his woman.

Winter Roses

Available November.

COMING NEXT MONTH

#1831 SECRETS OF THE TYCOON'S BRIDE—
Emilie Rose
The Garrisons
This playboy needs a wife and deems his accountant the perfect
bride-to-be...until her scandalous past is revealed.

#1832 SOLD INTO MARRIAGE—Ann Major
Can a wealthy Texan stick to his end of the bargain when he beds
the very woman he's vowed to blackmail?

#1833 CHRISTMAS IN HIS ROYAL BED—Heidi Betts
A scorned debutante discovers that the prince who hired her is the
same man who wants to make her his royal mistress.

#1834 PLAYBOY'S RUTHLESS PAYBACK—
Laura Wright
No Ring Required
His plan for revenge meant seducing his rival's innocent daughter.
But *is* she as innocent as he thinks?

#1835 THE DESERT BRIDE OF AL ZAYED—
Tessa Radley
Billionaire Heirs
She decided her secret marriage to the sheik must end...just as he
declared the time has come to produce his heir.

#1836 THE BILLIONAIRE WHO BOUGHT CHRISTMAS—
Barbara Dunlop
To save his family's fortune, the billionaire tricked his
grandfather's gold-digging fiancée into marriage. Now he
discovers he's wed the wrong woman!